SHORT STORIES by TEXAS AUTHORS

Short Stories & Poetry
by Texas Authors
Volume 9
© 2024 Texas Authors Institute
of History, Inc.
Cover Design by Bourgeois Media & Consulting

Limited Edition First Print 2024

ISBN 9798330323128
Published by Texas Authors Institute of History, Inc., a museum for Texas Authors, past, present and future.
http://TexasAuthors.Institute

Enter our Annual
Short Story Contest
Entries Accepted
March 1st to July 31st
each year.

TxShorts.com

Title	Author	Page

First Shots Fired in the Conquest of Texas

Conquest of Texas

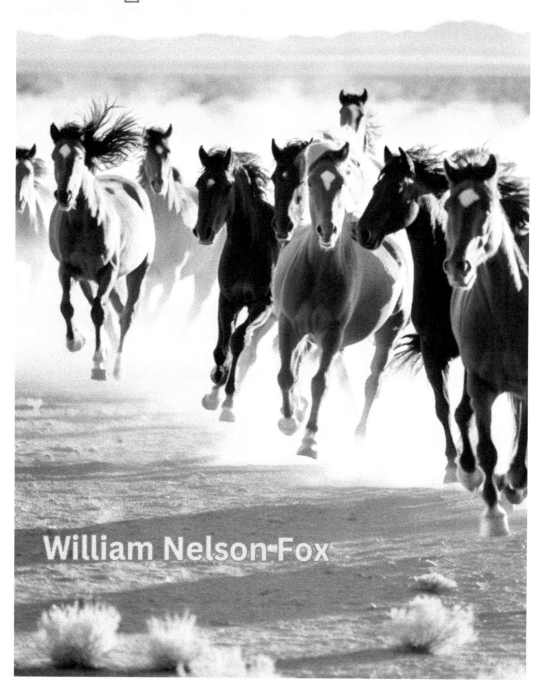

William Nelson Fox

First Shots Fired in the
Conquest of Texas
William Nelson Fox

Paranoid Spanish Texas authorities were suspicious of anyone crossing its border, especially Anglo-Americans. In Lower Louisiana, Spanish territorial officials reasoned that if they allowed new colonists in, they would be under direct Spanish rule, and they could be controlled. In Spanish Texas, provincial officials looked with disfavor at the entry of the Anglo-Americans, fearing that they would bring political discord and incite Texas Indians.

The best-known intruder who filtered into Texas was Philip Nolan. It is said that Nolan was small in stature, remarkably handsome, and had the demeanor of a gentleman, and he was famed for his extraordinary strength. He was a young Irish lad who worked for General James Wilkinson as his business shipping agent in New Orleans. However, after Wilkinson was forced to abandon his New Orleans commercial business and rejoined the army, Nolan needed another occupation. It was while working for Wilkinson that he heard of the trading opportunities in Texas.

Using the general's influence and ingratiating himself with Spanish officials, Nolan obtained a trading passport to enter Texas. The general had a unique relationship with Spanish officials in New Orleans –Wilkinson was a senior officer in the United States Army who was a paid Spanish spy known as Agent 13. Nolan handled much of Wilkinson's financial dealings with the Spanish.

Having obtained a trading passport and barely twenty years old, Nolan entered Texas. But Nolan's trading adventure didn't go as planned. Texas Spanish authorities refused to accept his Louisiana Spanish passport, accused him of being an American spy, and confiscated all of his trade goods.

Dejected but undeterred, Nolan made his way west to the Wichita Indian villages on the Red River, which acted as a trading post with Texas Indians. Because of the Indian trade with the

Americans, the Comanches built alliances with the Wichitas and peacefully visited their village. From the Wichita villages, Nolan traveled further west into the Texas interior, probably at the invitation of the Comanches. There, he went into seclusion, living the Indian life for two years, hunting and trapping animals. Nolan became an authority on the Indians, their culture, and their sign language.

All during this time, Nolan watched great herds of wild horses thundering by. A full-grown "wild mustang" was not large, lived off the grasses of the hot Texas plains and could go long distances between water holes. It would be these small Indian ponies that led to the saying: "A white man will ride the Mustang until he is played out; a Mexican will take him and ride him another day until he thinks he is played out; then a Comanche will mount him, and ride him to where he is going."

Living with the Indians, Nolan learned how to catch these wild horses. In late 1793 or early 1794, he ended his self-imposed exile in Spanish Texas and arrived unexpectedly back in New Orleans, driving fifty wild "mustang" horses. His reappearance amazed Louisiana Governor Carondelet, who believed Nolan had risen from the dead. Governor Carondelet gave Nolan another passport, and this time, his permit was for an official purpose - to secure horses for the Louisiana militia regiment.

Nolan made his second trip to Texas accompanied by five native Louisianans and a slave. His first stop was Nacogdoches, the gateway to the Texas frontier. With the aid of local residents, Nolan trapped animals. By November 1794, he had enough animal skins to bribe Spanish authorities and avoid any trouble. He traveled on to San Antonio de Bexar, the capital of the Texas province. In Bexar, he made the acquaintance of Texas Governor Manuel Munoz and obtained approval to trade in the province and capture wild horses.

In January 1796, Nolan rode home, this time with 250 horses. He sold the best in the growing American frontier regions where settlers and the U.S. Army were in great need of horses. By this time, Spanish officials in Texas had a watchful eye on Nolan. Nolan's intrusions had awakened Spanish authorities to Texas's vulnerability to outside intervention, particularly from the United States.

Meanwhile, Philip Nolan, preparing for his next venture into Texas, obtained yet another passport from Louisiana Governor

Carondelet. Apparently, even with Spanish suspicions, Nolan managed to patch things up, at least with Governor Carondelet in New Orleans. Besides giving Nolan a passport, Carondelet also wrote to Texas Governor Munoz on Nolan's behalf. Carondelet stated Nolan's importance to the royal service and wanted to secure him from any consequences.

Nolan departed on his third expedition into Texas, and this time, he took wagons loaded with trade goods. He arrived in San Antonio de Bexar in October 1797. However, unlike his first two visits, Nolan overstayed his welcome and immersed himself into Texas colonial society, managing not only to trade and collect horses but also to father a child. Nolan was named as the father of a girl, Maria Josefa, born out of wedlock on August 20, 1798, at San Antonio de Bexar to teenager Gertrudis Quinones.

As informants reported on Nolan's activities, Spanish officials grew more and more suspicious that Nolan's expeditions included more than the acquisition of horses. He covered too much Texas ground for the Spanish peace of mind. Nolan widely traveled central and north central Texas and knew the region better than the Spaniards did. Acquainted with astronomy and geography, Nolan spent a great deal of time exploring and making maps.

Thinking that Nolan had left the province in the summer of 1798, Commandant General Pedro de Nava in Chihuahua was alarmed to find Nolan still in Texas almost a year later. Texas Governor Munoz, who was in bad health, defended Nolan vigorously and claimed that his delay in removing Nolan was unavoidable. Only by the intercession of Munoz did Nolan escape the province, this time driving a herd, which was estimated to be between 1,000 and 2,500 horses, back to Natchez in late 1799.

After returning from his third expedition into Texas, Nolan married into a wealthy Natchez family, marrying twenty-one-year-old Fannie Lintot on December 19, 1799. Nolan was twenty-eight at the time. Fannie Lintot knew how famous Nolan was and that the ladies liked her husband. But unknown to her was that he already had two girlfriends and a child. One was the teenager Gertrudis Quinones of San Antonio de Bexar, who he had a daughter with a year before he married Fannie. His other lover, Gertrudis de Santos, was a fifty-year-old lady who lived in Nacogdoches. Gertrudis' husband, Antonio Leal, was a partner in Nolan's horse smuggling business. Nolan had visited Nacogdoches on his first trip into Texas and established a friendship with the Spanish resident and his very amiable wife, Gertrudis.

In August 1800, Juan Bautista de Elguezabal succeeded Manuel Munoz as the Spanish governor of Texas. Elguezabal feared the growing presence of Americans on Texas' eastern frontier. He ordered the arrest of anyone whose actions were suspect. Nolan was at the top of this list. The Texas governor believed that Nolan planned to encourage a revolution to overthrow Spanish rule in Texas. Elguezabal ordered the arrest and interrogation of Nolan should he enter Texas again. Spanish officials clearly regarded the young adventurer as "persona non grata."

Spanish agents in Natchez (on the American side) kept Jose Vidal, the Spanish Commandant at Post Concordia, across the Mississippi River from Natchez (on the Spanish side), informed of Nolan's activities. Vadal carried on the Spanish official's hostility toward Nolan. Nolan was playing different Spanish officials off against one another and was perceived as being involved with Americans who conspired to take New World territories from Spain. Commandant Vadal sent out warnings that if Nolan were not stopped, other Americans would follow.

Despite Commandant Vidal and other Spanish officials being on the lookout for another visit from the notorious horse trader, Philip Nolan prepared for yet another trip to Texas for mustangs, his fourth. Nolan was the only one in Natchez who had first-hand knowledge of the Spanish province to the west. Texas was an intriguing and unknown land.

To travel west across the Mississippi River into Spanish territory and on into Texas, one first had to obtain a passport from Commandant Vidal at the Post of Concord on the Spanish side of the Mississippi across from American Natchez. As Nolan prepared for his fourth trip west, he didn't bother to go through Vidal for a Spanish passport. With Nolan showing such contempt for Spanish authority, Vidal felt Nolan had to be captured and face justice. Vidal feared Nolan's disregard for Spanish law would encourage more Americans to enter Texas. Nolan had to be stopped from slipping in and out of Spanish territory.

Despite Nolan's awareness of Spanish attempts "to stop him," Nolan rode out of Natchez on November 1, 1800, this time with a well-armed party of twenty-eight. Most were Americans. Several were Spaniards. The majority were in their twenties, two were slaves, and one was in his mid-forties. Nolan was thirty.

Going north, and not south along the coast as he led the Spanish to believe, Nolan's party traveled up the Mississippi River to Nogales near present-day Vicksburg and then further north than necessary to evade detection by Spanish patrols. The party crossed the Mississippi River and headed west, crossing the Ouachita River near present-day Monroe and then across the Red River near present-day Shreveport.

Along the Red River, they visited the Caddo Indian villages, where Indians were friendly towards Nolan. Traveling on, the party came upon more Indians, Tawakonis, who were also friendly and who sold Nolan and his men fresh horses. In another six days, the party crossed the Trinity River, where the men found open prairies. They reached a creek called Painted Spring, so named because of a rock there that the Comanches had painted as a symbol of peace with other Indians.

In this vast Texas prairie country, there was no wood; the only fuel for a fire was buffalo dung, which lay dried on the ground in large quantities. Horse flesh was their only sustenance for nine days until they reached the Brazos River, where they found plenty of elk and deer, as well as some buffalo. It was there at the Brazos that they found wild horses by the thousands. This was Nolan's destination.

On the currently named Nolan River, a small tributary of the Brazos River, the mustangers constructed a log fort/corral, only five feet high and no roof. Local historians have disputed the exact location of Nolan's log fort, but in 1936, the state of Texas placed a granite historical marker near the present town of Blum in northwestern Hill Country.

From this fort/corral, Nolan's men rode on their mustang-catching forays. Experienced with a rope, Nolan knew how to cut a few hundred horses from a herd of thousands. He trained the others. Nolan and his men spent the winter catching horses, initially rounding up three hundred wild horses. During this time, Nolan held councils with various Indian tribes - the Tawakonis, Taovayas, and Comanches. The Indians also paid visits to Nolan's fort/corral, most likely to trade in horses.

A few days after catching the first three hundred wild horses, about two hundred Comanches, including men, women and children, came to visit the small encampment of white men. After their short visit, Nolan and most of the expedition members traveled with the Indians to the south fork of the Red River to visit the Comanche Chief Nicoroco. There, Nolan's men learned more about the horses they sought, as the Comanches were excellent horsemen and took great advantage of the mustangs they caught and tamed.

After spending about four weeks visiting with the Comanches, Nolan and his men returned to their camp near the Brazos River. Some of their Comanche hosts returned with Nolan to hunt for buffalo. When these Indians left Nolan's camp on their buffalo hunt, they took eleven horses, all gentle and trained. Without these trained horses, Nolan and his men could do nothing.

On discovering the theft, Nolan and five others immediately took off on foot after the thieving Indians. For nine days, the men walked in the cold of winter, searching for the Indians who had stolen the horses. Finally, they came upon a Comanche camp and found four men and a few women and children in the camp. They immediately recognized four of the stolen horses. An old Indian told them that the one who stole the horses had but one eye and that he and the other Comanches had gone out hunting buffalo and would return that evening. The Indians in the Comanche camp had a large quantity of buffalo meat drying and offered Nolan and his men some to eat, which the hungry men devoured and then rested.

That evening, "One-Eye" returned to camp. Nolan had him tied up and left him that way all night; the other Indians said nothing in protest. The next morning, after gathering their horses and taking all the buffalo meat that they could carry, Nolan and his men returned to their log fort/corral and continued to round up wild mustangs.

All the while, Spanish officials were becoming increasingly alarmed about Nolan's activities, thinking that Nolan was working to excite the "barbaric" Indian tribes against them. Additionally, they believed that Nolan's true mission was to deliver Texas to the hated North Americans by assisting those who wished to separate Texas from Spain. The Spanish were well aware of secret plots that were being hatched in the United States to seize Spanish lands.

All of this paranoia led Texas Governor Juan Elguezabal to order Spanish commandant Lieutenant Miguel Francisco Muzquiz in Nacogdoches to find and arrest Philip Nolan. Another person who was interested in the whereabouts of Philip Nolan was William Barr. The House of Barr and Davenport had an agreement with the Spanish government that gave them exclusive trading rights with Texas Indians. Nolan's presence in Texas threatened their business.

Lieutenant Muzquiz relied on Indian informants to put him on Philip Nolan's trail. After being informed of the general location of Nolan's camp, Lieutenant Muzquiz, with a Spanish force of approximately one hundred twenty soldiers and militia volunteers, a small swivel cannon, and a good supply of munitions, marched out from Nacogdoches on March 4, 1801, to find and arrest Philip Nolan. William Barr rode with the Spanish force to act as an interpreter between the Spanish and the Americans.

Muzquiz crossed the Trinity River on March 11, 1801, and found Nolan's camp at about 1:00 a.m. on March 20, 1801. Finally, the Spanish had Nolan in their grasp. Muzquiz positioned his little cannon to fire directly on Nolan's fort and waited for daylight. During the night, five of Nolan's men, who were supposed to be on guard, were captured outside the fort.

The nervous tramping of horses woke Nolan on Saturday morning, March 21, 1801. Just as the morning sun began to lighten the Texas horizon, Nolan peered over the wall of his roofless fort and saw scores of armed men. He knew why they were there. Nolan saw the dismay in the faces of his men as they faced the Spanish troops. Nolan had previously warned his men that if captured, they would face imprisonment for the rest of their lives. From the very outset, Nolan had told them always to be ready for a fight and to hang on long enough to mount an escape.

Nolan rode out for a consultation with Lieutenant Muzquiz. Not conversant in English, Muzquiz ordered his interpreter, William Barr, to tell Nolan and his men that he had come for the purpose of arresting them and that he expected them to surrender in the name of the King. Defiant, Nolan claimed that he had the governor's permit to collect horses. In the exchange, interpreter William Barr told Nolan that unless he had more men than he seemed to have, fighting was hopeless.

Returning to his little fort, Nolan and his men prepared to fight. Nolan reminded them that their ammunition was low and to make every shot count. The battle began with Muzquiz firing his little swivel cannon from a distance. It was easy fighting for Muzquiz - loading his little cannon with grapeshot and firing it pell-mell at the log fort. After ten minutes of firing, Nolan was killed. Some say he was killed by a discharge of grapeshot from the cannon; others say Nolan was slain by a musket ball that hit him in the head.

At about 9:00 a.m., with Nolan dead and two men wounded, Nolan's men did just what Nolan had asked them to do; they attempted to escape. They loosened the logs on the fort's side opposite the firing cannon. Each man filled his powder horn and gave the remaining stock of powder to Caesar, one of Nolan's slaves who did not have a gun to carry. After the cannon's next discharge, the men, including the two wounded men, made for the woods behind the fort, leaving behind the body of their brave commander.

For a few minutes, their retreat was not noticed, but the silence from the log/fort alerted Muzquiz, and he realized that his quarry had fled. Muzquiz's ordered his men to give chase. As the mustangers fled, Caesar, who was carrying all of the mustangers' extra supply of powder, lagged behind and was caught. Also, one of the wounded men, who could not keep up with his friends, stopped. He was surrounded and became a prisoner.

For six hours, the mustangers were pursued, stopping only to fire and then retreating again. This firing and retreating went on until the escaping men had empty powder horns. David Fero walked out of the deep ravine where Nolan's men had last stopped. He walked up to Musquiz and handed the Spanish lieutenant his knife and guns. One by one, the others followed, surrendering their arms.

Lieutenant Muzquiz promised the Americans that if they agreed to never return to Texas, they would be sent back to Natchez. The Americans agreed and became prisoners in the hands of a nation known for its brutality to prisoners, just what Nolan had warned against. Ceasar and Robert, both slaves, asked permission to bury their master, which Muzquiz granted, but not before having Philip Nolan's ears cut off in order to send them to the Governor of Texas. William Barr carried the gruesome tokens to the governor as proof that Nolan was dead.

The next day, the Americans and the Spanish troops started for Nacogdoches, the only Spanish outpost in East Texas. However, when they arrived in Nacogdoches, instead of escorting them onto the border and allowing them to return to the United States as they had been promised, Nolan's men were condemned for violations of Spanish law. The mustangers were put in irons and sent off under a strong guard to San Antonio de Bexar. From that moment on, the words Spanish honor has meant in Texas "a snare and a lie."

With Nolan dead and his men sent off to prison, extensive testimony was taken by the Spanish authorities to determine the true motives for Nolan's expedition. Most of Nolan's men swore that they entered Texas to help their leader bring out horses. No one professed any knowledge of a "scheme of conquest." This did not satisfy their Spanish inquisitors, and more relentless examinations were conducted on Nolan's suspected collaborators. Those arrested and interrogated included Gertrudis de los Santos and her husband, Antonio Leal; both were believed to have helped Nolan in his horse smuggling business.

Antonio Leal was a rancher in San Antonio de Bexar, where Nolan met him in 1790. Land owned by Leal and his wife (later known as the Edmund Quirk grant, on which San Augustine was built) was used for collecting and pasturing Nolan's horses before they were sent on into Louisiana. Spanish interrogation of Gertrudis and her husband included Gertrudis' rumored *mala amistad* (illicit affair). As it turns out, Gertrudis' lover was, in fact, Nolan. According to one informant, everyone knew about Gertrudis' illegitimate relations with the trader. When Antonio Leal was asked what his wife did for Nolan, he responded that he did not know what his wife did in assisting Nolan or where they traveled together because he was absent trading with the Tonkawas.

Despite being from among the wealthier families in Spanish East Texas, Gertrudis de Santos and Antonio Leal acted like many others on the borderland, welcoming relations with outsiders in order to extend kinship ties and economic opportunities. Antonio Leal and his wife were taken from Nacogdoches to San Antonio de Bexar and put on trial for their alleged part in the Nolan intrigue. At the end of the trial, Spanish authorities exiled them to Coahuila.

After three months, the captured mustangers were placed in irons and marched south into Mexico, first to Saltillo, then to San Luis Potosi, and eventually to Chihuahua, where they arrived on March 14, 1803. Nolan's associates were to be held in Chihuahua until the King's pleasure regarding them was known. This took time under the snail-paced Spanish system. At first, they were kept in irons and cruelly treated; then their irons were removed, and they were permitted to walk about the town, but they had to return at night to sleep in military barracks.

First Shots Fired

In April 1807, Zebulon Pike arrived in Chihuahua after having been found in Spanish territory and was brought to Chihuahua to be questioned. While there, under a loose form of house arrest, Pike was actually treated with considerable hospitality. David Fero heard that Pike was in town and left his presidio of confinement for a clandestine meeting with Pike. Fero had served as Pike's father's aide-de-camp when he was younger. Fero, with tears in his eyes, told Pike of the circumstances of the prisoners and that most were well; they were fearful of execution. Fero asked Pike to notify their families and friends about their situations. Pike promised to do so.

Upon his return to the United States, Pike fulfilled his promise to Fero. At Natchitoches, Pike penned a letter to the *Natchez Herald* on the status of Nolan's men in Mexico, which the paper published on August 10, 1807. Pike listed the names of the prisoners and provided what little information he knew about each. He called the imprisoned men "debilitated and half-lost wretches." He asked the *Herald* to inform newspapers in other states where some of the men had family and friends. Until this time, nothing had been known of Nolan and his men's fate. This news caused a stir in Natchez as most considered it an outrage that the men had been imprisoned.

A ruling issued by Spain finally arrives in Mexico. The verdict was that two men who fought until capture were to be executed, and the rest imprisoned for ten years. The Spaniards had already held the men for over six years, and all but nine had died in prison or escaped. So, it was decided that one man was to be chosen to die for bearing arms against Spanish authority. The mustangers were assembled in the Plaza de Los Urgangas in Chihuahua to determine their fate. They were made to kneel in front of a drum. On the drum was a glass tumbler. Two dice were placed in the tumbler. Each man had to make a roll; the man with the lowest number faced execution. Ephraim Blackburn rolled a "3" and "1", making "four," which proved to be the lowest number, and it sealed his fate.

On Wednesday, November 11, 1807, two days after throwing the unlucky "four," with sorrowful hearts, Blackburn's companions watched as his body dropped through the trap. The remaining men were marched south to spend the rest of their lives in prison in Mexico.

Philip Nolan is often credited as the first Anglo-American

cowboy in Texas, the first Anglo-American to map Texas, and some believe he was the first in a long line of filibusters to free Texas from Spanish rule. Nolan passed his maps and observations on to his mentor, General James Wilkinson. Some historians believe Nolan met with Thomas Jefferson, who was then vice president. Jefferson wrote a letter to Nolan on January 24, 1798, inquiring about "wild horses in the country west of Louisiana." Some historians think that they did meet, although a meeting remains undocumented. Nolan, being a person with first-hand knowledge of the Texas Spanish province, causes some to think that a great deal more than the habits of wild horses were discussed, given the United States's government and Jefferson's interest in Texas. After the meeting, This would have been before Nolan's fourth expedition into Texas.

Other questions have been raised. Why were the Spanish so keen on stopping Philip Nolan? Trading in Texas was illegal but most often winked at by Spanish frontier officials who saw an opportunity to line their pockets. Was Nolan spying for General James Wilkinson? Why did Nolan keep his journal so carefully? Why did he map Texas? Why did he and David Fero, Nolan's second in command, mark so carefully the distances and courses of their routes?

Some readers may be aware of a fiction story borrowing Philp Nolan's name, *A Man Without A Country*, written by Edward Everett Hale, about a U.S. army lieutenant convicted of treason and spent his life at sea; however, the "real" Philp Nolan lived decades before, entered Texas for wild mustang horses, and was killed in a fight in Texas.

Was the "real" Philip Nolan just smuggling horses for profit? Was he the first American to filibuster in Texas? In any case, Nolan's legacy is noted in early official U.S. government maps. Captain Zebulon Montgomery Pike explored and mapped much of the western United States soon after Nolan's death. Pike's map of the *Internal Province of New Spain* was published in 1807. In the area marked "Province of Texas," there are hundreds of miles left without any features north of San Antonio to the Red River. These open ranges are marked as having "Immense Herds of Wild Horses."

Nolan's death did not stop others from entering Texas. The first shots in the conquest of Texas had been fired! There would be more fights between Americans and the Spanish before Texas becomes American.

First Shots Fired

Why I Wrote This Story
Texas's 1800s history is filled with adventurous experiences, dramatic incidents, and memorable events that shaped the Texas that we know today. It is a period filled with people, places, and events like the Alamo and San Jacinto in 1836. But even before that, earlier Texas is a period of numerous intrigues involving an unknown land. This story at the turn of the century gives the reader a better understanding of the "real" Philip Nolan's legacy in Texas history.

Survivor
Marsha R. West

Least Likely to Succeed. That's the honor her class had bestowed on her in their 1994 yearbook. Robyn Hawthorn couldn't argue with their assessment. She'd spent years in therapy after spending years in the drunk tanks of various small towns, hooking up with losers like herself. While both her parents had been drunks of one kind or another, therapy had taught her going down that road had been entirely her choice. As much as she hated that, she accepted she'd made that choice.

Life was all about choices. Like now. She'd chosen to attend the 30th reunion of their high school class in Dallas. Reasons to make the decision varied. Admittedly, she wanted people to see how she'd turned out. She hadn't stayed the class loser. Mainly she needed to see Brett Jackson again. The boy who'd raped her when they'd been in 10th grade. An act which contributed to her downward spiral of drink and self-hatred. She especially wanted him to see he hadn't won. Oh he almost won. She'd earned the title the class bestowed on her. And probably hurt folks in the process.

She especially hoped to see Steve Handley. The kindest person she'd ever known. He reached out to her during the worst parts of her senior year. She kept blowing him off. She wasn't good enough for him. What had he been thinking to try to befriend the class lush? He took some heat for that, too. She owed him an apology and a thank you.

As for the girls? The cheerleaders and soccer players? She'd never been close to any of them except blonde, blue-eyed Lilly Standish who'd tried to befriend Robyn, but again, she'd blown off that sweet girl. Lilly kept trying to get Robyn to play soccer. But that took strength and stamina. Neither of which Robyn had. Drink stole all of that from her. She'd been scrawny then too. Not enough healthy food and exercise. The idea of being able to say thank you to Lilly filled Robyn with joy. Lilly's efforts had been appreciated then, and they still were. Because she'd reached out to Robyn, Lilly also took some guff from the other girls. Girls who saw nothing of redeeming value in the lush.

Who knew if those three people would attend. Even after she became sober and got her life together, she'd never gone to any of the other reunions the class held. She finished college with a degree in psychology and went on to earn a Master's in Counseling. Now she worked in a small clinic with kids who struggled with the same kinds of issues she had. Her hope was to help them choose to turn around their lives before they hit rock bottom the way she had. Supporting them in their efforts gave her life purpose.

Robyn took one last glance in the full length mirror hanging on the closet door of her room in the fancy downtown hotel where the reunion dinner and dance would take place. Her shoulder length soft brown hair brushed the tops of her shoulders. She wore the few streaks of gray as a badge of her survival. Not scrawny anymore either. The sleeveless, black sequined sheath dress showed off her curves and stopped at her knees. The V-neck hinted at her cleavage. It had taken her a long time to be willing to show even that much, fearing some other guy would see it as a come-on and attack her. To accept she was not at fault for what had happened. The black high heels gave added height to her short stature. And yes, they made her legs look good.

Picking up her black sequined bag, she nodded once to her image. "Let's do this."

Riding down in the elevator, her heart rate kicked up. How would this evening go? Would she regret coming? Would she find the specific people she wanted to see? And would she find the right words to say what she intended?

The elevator doors opened to the sounds of a band coming from the ballroom. She swallowed twice, wet her lips, and marched toward the table in front of the main ballroom doors. Three women dressed in colorful sparkly dresses sat behind the white covered table with lists and badges spread out in front of them. Robyn chose the line on the left behind a couple she didn't recognize. But then that wasn't surprising. It was a class of two hundred and fifty students. She didn't know even half that. Finally it was her turn.

A blonde woman looked up with a smile plastered on her

face. "Hey, welcome." She studied Robyn a moment. "I'm sorry, I don't recognize you. We had such a large class. What's your name?"

"Robyn Hawthorne." Proud her voice showed no hint of the trembles threatening to undo her core.

"Oh. I think I remember seeing your name here." She ran her finger down the names on the page in front of her. "Yes, here you are." Her gaze flicked between the picture on the name badge and the woman in front of her. Finally, she put a check mark by Robyn's name and handed her a name badge suspended from green and purple ribbons. "And you get two drink tickets."

"Thank you." Robyn took the tickets and the ribbon with a picture of the girl she'd once been and slid it over her head and around her neck, fluffing out her hair. "Can you tell me if Lilly Standish, Steve Handley, and Brett Jackson are attending tonight?"

"Sure I can check that out for you." The woman took a moment to scan the pages in front of her. "Yes, all three of them have already checked in. They're not assigned to your table for dinner, which is number 20. Just mill around and you'll probably run into them."

"I will. Thank you." As Robyn walked off the women's voices followed her. "Can you believe that was Robyn Hawthorne?...I'm surprised she even came…Boy, she sure looks different."

As she entered the ballroom, Robyn walked tall—as tall as she could at 5'2 inches maybe tonight hitting 5'5" with the crazy heels she'd splurged on for the event. She paused and let her gaze slide around the room. The dimmed lights made it difficult for her to recognize people.

A giant dragon mascot stood on the left side of the room underneath an arch created from green and purple balloons and streamers. It seemed to be set up for pictures. Not something she'd do. A pale green banner stretched across the stage with purple letters spelling out: Metroplex High School Class of 1994 Reunion. She'd actually arrived.

The ballroom was suitably decked out with a dozen or so round tables covered with white tablecloths. Yellow containers sat in the center of the tables filled with small, purple flowers. Nice they weren't tall. It would make talking easier. Not that Robyn anticipated sitting at her table. A dance floor was directly in front of the stage and numerous couples were dancing. Two bars lined the rear and right walls of the ballroom.

Now to find Brett, Steve, and Lilly. After that she could leave. Hopefully, she'd find them before dinner began. Brett had been a football player, well over six and a half feet tall and strong. He'd been one of the biggest guys on the team. It should be easy to find him. He was the guy who took over the whole sidewalk, never giving a thought to someone coming toward him. Assuming they'd get out of his way. And generally they did. Robyn's eyes scanned the tops of the heads of people. She didn't see anyone exceptionally tall. Perhaps he hadn't arrived yet.

Making her way to the bar on the right side of the ballroom, she moved around several small groups of people over-hearing their talk.

"So glad you came."

"You haven't changed at all."

"What cute kids." As someone shared pictures.

"Did you see Sylvia? Wow, she's gained so much weight! Would never have expected that!"

"Oh, yes. I've done well. I'm Vice President for operations at Timbercreek Lumber, get to travel all over."

"You have three homes? You have done well for yourself."

Finally, it was her turn.

"What can I get you, ma'am?" The bartender asked.

"Do you have sparkling water?"

"Sure do. Plain or with lime?"

"Lime please." In moments the young man handed her a tall slim glass of bubbles with a straw sticking out and a napkin. "Thank you." Robyn handed him one of her drink tickets and eased to the side as another person shouldered his way to the bar. She raised her gaze. Well, I'll be. Brett had stood right behind her. Moving several steps to the left, she let her gaze sweep over him. As tall as she remembered and still broad shouldered, but he'd definitely added a paunch.

She didn't need or want an audience when she talked with him. Her intent wasn't to embarrass him or cause him trouble. Just to make him aware she had survived him.

Carrying a beer he walked away from the bar. Robyn followed him at a distance sipping her fizzy water. He stopped near three other men. They slugged each other on the arm and basically acted like they were still in high school. Lots of raucous laughter with a few muttered curse words. Brett finished his beer, hitched up his pants, and lumbered for the far side of the ballroom. Robyn trailed behind as he strutted into the hall and made for the men's room. She noted the balding spot on the back of his head and didn't repress a grin. He must hate that.

After setting her glass on an empty try, she leaned against the wall across from the restroom and waited for him. Brett exited the restroom and strode toward the ballroom. She drew in a deep breath and stepped in front of him, making him stop. "Hello, Brett."

"Hi." The man stared at her. His gaze traveled from the top of her head to the tip of her sparkly heels and back again. A smile spread across his face. "I can't say I recognize you, but I'd sure like to get to know you, pretty lady. Please tell me you're not here with one of my classmates. Hey, even if you are, we could go someplace quiet and get to know each other." One arm reached toward her, and his hand brushed up and down her arm.

She repressed a shudder and refused to pull away from him. "Brett, I'm Robyn Hawthorne."

Still his gaze was blank.

"Think back to our sophomore year. Out behind the bleachers late one Thursday night."

His eyes blinked rapidly. Again his gaze ran up and down her body, but this time she could tell when he placed her. "Robyn?"

"I don't know if you remember, but you raped me that night."

"Shut up. Keep your voice down." His head swiveled to see if anyone stood nearby. "I did no such thing. Besides, you wanted it as much as I."

His logic defied reason. "No, I didn't. I said no. I said stop. I may have been drunk, but you ignored my words and took what you wanted. You didn't cause me to become a lush, but you contributed to it."

His gaze continued to roam her body. "Well, you don't look much like a lush now."

"Thanks, I guess."

"What do you want?" One hand in his pants pocket nervously jangled change, and he looked around again to make sure they were alone.

"I don't want anything except to tell you, I survived you. And I forgive you."

"You forgive me? Get over yourself, woman. You wanted it

as much as I did. You probably never had it better."

Robyn drew in a deep breath. "That's all I needed to say, Brett. Have a good evening." She angled away from him. Her heels clicked on the tile floor as she walked across the hall and into the ballroom. Pausing inside, she clenched her hands and released them. She'd done what she needed to do. One down two to go.

Now to find Lilly and Steve. Robyn sidled up to a small group of women. "Excuse me. I'm looking for Lilly Standish. Have any of you seen her?"

A woman whose name tag said she was Patty Holcomb Jennings, smiled at Robyn. "Yes. I saw her checking out the buffet tables." She pointed to the left side of the room. "Lilly's on the planning committee, you know, and I'm sure she wants to make sure everything is perfect."

"Thank you." Robyn drifted off in the direction of the mascot and the serving tables.

Words from the group followed her as she walked away: "Her name tag said Robyn Hawthorne, but that couldn't be she, could it? She's a knockout."

Robyn didn't suppress her smile. Yeah, she was proud of how she'd turned herself around. Not by herself and not like it had been easy, by any means. Reaching the buffet table she spotted Lilly, at least, she suspected that's who the slim, attractive blonde woman was who walked between the two long tables. As the woman came to the end of her inspection, Robyn caught up with her. "Lilly, do you have a moment?"

The woman faced her with a smile on her face, "Sure. What can I do for you?" She automatically read the name tag and then her gaze flicked up and down coming back to Robyn's eyes. "Oh, my God, Robyn. You look fantastic. I'm so glad you're here." Surprising the heck out of Robyn, Lilly reached out and wrapped her arms around her in a giant hug. Robyn returned the embrace and then stepped back.

"Lilly, I came so I could say, thank you." Robyn still held one of Lilly's hands.

"Thank me? Whatever for?"

"See. isn't that just like you? I want to thank you for always being nice to me and trying to include me when we were in high school. I'm sorry, I wasn't in a place to respond."

"What happened to you after we graduated? You didn't stay

in Dallas?"

"No, I moved around a lot. I ended up in San Marcos and after many years went to college there."

"Well, where have you been? What are you doing? And let me say again how fantastic you look."

Robyn chuckled. "Well, thank you. Getting off the booze really helps improve your life."

"Oh, I suspect you have quite a story to tell. I always wondered what happened, and I worried about you."

"Thanks, Lilly. That means a lot. You haven't seen Steve Handley have you? He's the other person I really wanted to see. He was always kind to me."

"Yeah, I saw him earlier. He served on the planning committee along with me and about eight other people."

"Y'all have done a really good job. The decorations look great, and this buffet smells divine."

A woman came up to them. "Excuse me. Lilly, are we about ready to start people through the lines?"

"Yes, we are. Becky, you remember Robyn Hawthorne, don't you?"

Becky glanced at her name tag and appeared to force a smile. "Sure. Hey. Glad you came. You look good."

"Thanks, Becky. I'm glad to be here." And she was. She'd feel even better as soon as she talked with Steve. Then she'd retreat upstairs and order room service. She'd have accomplished what she came to do.

"Ladies and gentlemen, let me have your attention."

At the sound of the deep voice over the mic, Robyn turned toward the stage. There he was. Steve Handley. Of course, the master of ceremonies. He wore a dark suit and a white shirt with a purple tie. She'd read up on him and learned he was a local TV station newscaster. His dark hair, as thick as she remembered was now highlighted with streaks of gray. He wore it in a short style.

"Welcome to the 1994 Metroplex High School Reunion. We're so glad you could be with us tonight. I want to take a minute to thank our planning committee." He listed off the ten names, some Robyn even recognized. Applause was loud and the cheers raucous. "Hope you've found your tables. We're ready to begin serving, and we'll go numerically beginning with tables one through four. There are two serving tables and you can be on each side. I'll give you a heads up when it's time for the next four tables to go. Right now, Reverend Bill Blair will lead us in an invocation.

That Bill had become a minister didn't surprise Robyn, nor did she figured anyone else. His prayer was short and to the point, and laughter and chatting immediately followed the "Amens." Robyn strolled toward the stairs on the right side of the stage to catch Steve when he came down.

"Steve, I know you're busy, but I'd love just a few minutes of your time." Robyn's hand tightened on the thin black strap of her purse.

"Sure." He stepped away from the stairs, and his eyes grew large. "Robyn? Will you look at you?" He took both her hands, drew her close, and kissed her cheek. I saw your name on the attendance list and hoped to find you so we could have a good catching up."

A warmth grew in Robyn's middle at his generous welcome. "You're busy, Stan. I won't take long. I just wanted to say thank you for being so kind to me when we were in high school. I'm sorry I couldn't hear what you kept telling me and showing me. But I'm okay now and have been for some time." She turned to go, but he clung to her hand.

"Wait. I want more time. What table is yours?"

"Twenty, but I'm not staying. I've seen the people I wanted to."

"No please, I want to know what you're doing now. You must be doing well because you look gorgeous."

Warmth filled Robyn's cheeks, and she figured they turned a rosy hue. "That's so kind, Steve. Just like you always were."

"Not kind, Robyn, just stating a fact." His eyes darted to the serving tables. "Please don't leave. I've got to tell the next groups to get in line. Promise you'll stay."

Robyn found herself nodding. Not sure why but compelled to do what he'd asked her.

His deep voice boomed from the mike. "Okay, let's have tables five through eight go through the serving lines. In fact, why don't you keep an eye out on your own. When these guys are about halfway through the line, the next tables can go on up. I trust you to not get into any scuffling matches." Laughter roared from the audience. Steve hurried down the stairs and rejoined Robyn.

"They can manage on their own, and we can have some time

to ourselves."

"Should you have done that?"

"Sure why not? It's good to be flexible in life and go with what's most important. And right now, that's you." He took her by the hand and led her outside the ballroom, drawing her down on one of the cushioned settees in the hallway. "Not as loud out here. Do you know I searched for you?"

"You did? Why?"

"You were having a tough time our senior year, and I worried about you." He kept hold of her hand. "So tell me everything. Are you married? Do you have kids? Where do you live and what do you do?"

Robyn laughed. "That's a lot. I've been married several times, but I'm not currently married. No kids. I live in San Marcos and work in a small counseling office seeing high school kids, many of whom struggle with alcohol just the way I did."

"Wow. That's super. I'm so happy for you."

"What about you, Steve. Married?" Gosh she hoped not with him still holding her hand which she admitted felt really good.

"I'm a widower, Robyn, for about five years now. My wife Alice had breast cancer and fought it hard, but in the end Cancer won."

"I'm so sorry. That must've been so difficult."

"It wasn't any fun, but we had a good life even through the worst times. I have two kids, a son and a daughter. They both live in Dallas, not far from where I do. Not a grandfather yet but looking forward to that time. I keep busy with the TV station. They were good to me when Alice was sick, and let me cut back my hours, so now I work extra hard for them."

"They're lucky to have you. You've always had a great voice."

"You think I have a great voice, do you?" a smile quirked up one side of his mouth.

"Well, yes. I remember how well you did the announcements when we were in high school. Where'd you go to school?"

"Texas. Got jobs in some of the smaller venues and over time worked my way up into the DFW market."

"Good for you." Robyn stood, but he still held her hand. "Steve, I need to go. And you've got a reunion to continue ram rodding."

He stood. "Please stay, Robyn." He grasped both of her hands

29

in his. "I don't want us to lose this connection. You feel it too, don't you. Please say you do." His piercing brown gaze speared hers. She couldn't turn away.

What could she say? If she were honest, she'd say yes. But that wasn't the purpose of her coming to the reunion. It was just to say her thanks to Lilly and Steve and to show Brett she'd survived him.

She'd done those things, but oh, she yearned to respond to Steve's request.

"Robyn, at least give me your contact info so we can get together after tonight. Don't pull a Cinderella on me."

Robyn laughed. "Okay, I give. What's your cell number, and I'll text you, so you have mine."

He gave her his number, and she texted him. "There, we're connected." Robyn slid her phone back into her small purse.

"Robyn Hawthorn, I promise I will be in touch. I want to see a lot more of you and hear about your life. I want you to meet my kids, too."

"Oh my goodness, Steve."

"Don't let me scare you, but this is too important to let this moment get by us." He leaned close, slid both hands up to her cheeks and kissed her. The most tender, and yet passionate kiss of her life. When he pulled away, Robyn felt sad, but also incredibly hopeful. So this was why she'd survived.

The end.

Why I Wrote this Story

I wrote this short story two summers ago while our family was on vacation in Red River, New Mexico, getting away from a brutal Texas summer. Because I write "Later in Life Romance," I set the story at a 30th high school school reunion to fit the theme my writing chapter set for an anthology which unfortunately never was published. I like the idea that we have more than one opportunity to get our life on the right path. My husband gave me a plaque that says what my books and stories show: "Everything will be all right in the end. If it's not all right, it's not the end." If you like this story, you might want to check out my website for links to my books. **MarshaRWest.com**

B J Butt

FOR THE MOST PART

a story

For the Most Part
B J Butt

Once upon a time there was a man named Max. On the great scale of life, Max weighed in as a good man. Not an exceptional man, not an excellent man, but a good one, for the most part.

He graduated from his small-town high school at the top of his class. The same year man walked on the moon, Uncle Sam called upon eighteen year old Max to fight for American values in a small Asian country on the South China Sea. He joined the Marines and served until he was released from the North Vietnamese Army's "Hanoi Hilton" POW camp in the spring of '73. Max was lucky, he'd only been captive five months. Upon his return to civilian life, Max took advantage of the Army's promise to pay for higher education. After getting a Bachelor of Science in engineering, he continued his studies for two more years and earned a master's degree. He had his pick of jobs. Accepted one with a six-figure salary, great benefits and a future that was open wide. Thirty years old and his American dream had finally come true.

But that didn't stop the nightmares.

The brutality he'd seen from the Viet Cong, who took no prisoners, and the inhumane treatment by the NVA camp visited horrors upon him in his sleep. He could no longer believe that all the actions he took against the enemy were in defense of his country. But more than that, he experienced the deprivation and torture he'd endured in the camp, over and over again. His body would always bear the scars. As would his soul. Nine nights out of ten he woke shaking and screaming in a cold sweat. He moved through his days like a somnambulist, afraid to fully awaken, afraid that Epiales could somehow overcome sleep and visit his demon visions upon Max's conscious mind.

Then he found another kind of a dream. Her name was Camilla.

For the Most Part

Camilla captured his senses, filled his mind and heart so fully that she pushed the troublesome memories right out of his head. She was the cure, his balm of Gilead. Her palliative love healed his brokenness. He couldn't believe this beautiful angel loved him, wanted him. His better half, she completed him, made him whole.

And through everything that happened, all the way to the end, she'd kept him whole. She'd kept his demons at bay.

He remembered the day they first heard the diagnosis. "Alzheimer's," the doctor said. Max's brow furrowed, he gazed at his wife of fifteen years and clasped her cold hand. "How can that be, doc?" he'd asked. "She's only thirty-nine. Our youngest child is still in elementary school."

"I'm aware. It's very unusual. But I can find no other reason for the memory lapses and periods of disorientation. We've conducted test after test over the last two years. We've watched as her mental function has diminished. Research labs are working on it, but there's no true diagnostic test for Alzheimer's yet. Nevertheless, it's what best fits her symptoms, I'm sorry."

"But . . . but it could be something else. Right? I mean, there must be some tests we haven't tried. Um, like . . . screening her blood for heavy metals or pesticides or . . ."

"I suppose anything's possible. Look, I don't want to give you false hope. You said yourself that her lapses are becoming more frequent. Clinical assessments of her cognitive abilities show steady decline." The doctor shifted his attention to Camilla. She blinked impossibly long lashes, lifted her face and met his eye. "We've ruled out cancer, heart disease, poison, allergies." A shadow of a smile crossed her face. "Though I still think there might be some immune system response that's causing—" Slowly, she swept an invisible hair behind her ear and lowered her gaze. He stared at her for a long moment, then sighed. "Okay, let's keep looking. In the meantime, there's a new medication I'd like her to try."

She quit her job. The doctor thought reducing stress would help her immune system to focus on the problem in her brain, with the additional benefit of her not being exposed to every germ that came in off the street harbored by her coworkers.

For a while, it worked. She was able to drive the children to school and their lessons. She volunteered at the library and took a class in photography.

Max thought they had beaten it, whatever it was. Thought his love had cured her, just like hers had cured him. Then came the awful day when he arrived home from work to find the house a disaster, the kids nowhere to be seen and Camilla on her hands and knees scrubbing the kitchen floor, stark naked. At his approach she sat back on her heels and pointed the scrub brush at him. "Don't you dare step on my clean tiles. Don't you dare."

He decided it was time to take the children along on the next doctor visit. They were old enough. They should know. Delia was almost thirteen. She'd just crossed that threshold into womanhood. She needed a mother's guidance. Jaxon would be sixteen next month. They needed to know. He needed them to know. He needed them to know everything.

The doctor recited an appropriately detailed history, diagnosis and prognosis of their mother's condition.

Delia sniffled. The doctor pushed a box of tissues across his desk to her. She grabbed one and wiped her eyes. "You said you didn't reach this diagnosis quickly or easily but ruled out a lot of other things first. What kinds of other things?" His daughter always had a question.

Max found her a disappointment and a surprise. On the day of her birth, he'd been disappointed that she hadn't inherited her mother's genes, but instead looked just like him. He'd been surprised when she turned out to be beautiful anyway.

"Ah yes, well," said the doctor. "We started with a complete physical exam . . ."

Max tuned him out. He'd heard it all before. He could tell the doctor felt more comfortable talking medicine than feelings.

"And lastly Post Traumatic Stress Disorder."

Delia continued her interrogation. "Mental illness? Could something like this be psychological?"

Mental illness? Max knew PTSD well. Camilla had been part of his recovery from the flashbacks and tremors. Heck, she'd been the cure. But mental illness? He hadn't been crazy.

"The impact of the mind on the body's health shouldn't be underestimated. Post Traumatic Stress Disorder is very real. Sometimes people block out conscious memories that are too stressful to cope with. And once they start blocking memories, who knows where it will stop. There are all sorts of things the mind can do that science doesn't have answers for."

"How about a physical injury?"

"Certainly possible. A lesion, contusion or structural impairment may lead to brain damage and dementia. But there's no record of her suffering a blow to the head severe enough to call for hospitalization. Nothing showed up on her EEG or x-rays."

"Could it be genetic?" This from Jaxon.

"It doesn't appear to be anywhere else in your family history . . . that I know of." The doctor nodded his head at Max. "We went back several generations. I doubt it's got anything to do with your genes."

"But it could." Jax refused to back down.

"Theoretically, anything is possible. But the probability is very low."

Delia gave her brother a withering look. "Worried about yourself, are you?" She turned to the doc. "Can you help her? I mean, I know she isn't going to get better, but—"

"Hey! I'm right here." Camilla finally joined the conversation after sitting motionless and staring off into space for the most of it.

The doctor reached across his desk and patted Delia's hand, but his eyes locked with Camilla's as he said, "I'll do all I can. I promise."

All he could turned out to be not much. Six months later Max took early retirement so he could stay home with Camilla full time. The kids needed him there too. Not some nanny. They'd continue to be together, a family. It would just be a little different now. Fortunately, money wasn't a problem. Max managed their stock portfolio and worked on a new patent idea when he wasn't taking care of Camilla.

Somehow, they got through the next few years. Jaxon pleased Max by choosing to attend college at his alma mater. Jax couldn't wait to leave. It was an out of state school. All the way across the country wouldn't have been far enough for him. Delia was resentful. Caring for her demented mother wasn't high on her list of fun things to do. And once Jaxon left for school, her burden doubled. When Max wasn't bathing Camilla, or dressing Camilla, or feeding Camilla, or soothing Camilla, he was fighting with his daughter.

It was getting to be too much. But he'd never put his wife in a home. Never. Unlike her mind, her beauty hadn't dimmed. He saw the way the doctor looked at her even now. He'd never let them have her. Still, it was hard. There were days when he thought about ending it all. Her suffering. His. He had a gun. Two bullets were all it'd take.

But she was his wife. His beloved wife and the mother of his children. He had to keep it together, even if it seemed impossible at times.

It'd been an especially rough day with Camilla. Max had started drinking in the early afternoon, to steady his nerves. His lips were ship-sinkers by the time dinner rolled around.

"I know what it was," he slurred and took another sip of bourbon. He wondered when he had quit bothering with ice.

"What 'what' was, Dad?" Jaxon was in town. He looked taller and more filled out. Older. Wiser? No. More cynical, perhaps.

"The trauma . . ." Max looked at the meal before him, hiccupped and felt bile rise in his throat.

Delia had cooked dinner, sausage in bottled barbecue sauce with box macaroni and powdered orange cheese plus plain microwaved frozen mixed vegetables. She'd gone to the trouble to bake some blueberry muffins from a bag mix.

Max couldn't help but remember the succulent homemade stroganoff with tender beef and fresh mushrooms and the creamy crawfish bisque Camilla used to make. He missed *that* Camilla. He took another slug of the bourbon before he said, "The trauma your mother— The thing what made her— The reason she'sh the way she is."

"Is that right?" Delia looked at her brother, pursed her lips and rolled her eyes.

"Yesh. She had an affair. With . . . with a woman."

"What are you talking about?" Delia's voice was shrill.

"Get out." Jaxon pushed back in the chair and crossed his meaty arms. "You're kidding."

"No. No, it's true. She confessed to me," he slurred. "She cried and cried, certain she would be going to Hell for this transgression. I told her God would forgive her. That Jesus died for her sins. But she felt so guilty for being unfaithful to me. That was the guilt that traumatized her, breaking her marriage vow to me. She couldn't let it go. That's what made her sick."

Jaxon shook his head. "Oh, c'mon, Dad. You're drunk. I don't believe you. Mom would never."

Fire raged in Delia's eyes. "Do you really think you were so important to her that Mom would give us up?" She pointed to Jaxon and herself. "Give up her whole life over being unfaithful to you?"

"Yesh," Max cleared his throat. He made an effort to sober his speech. "Yes, she would. Of course, she would. We . . . our love . . ."

Jaxon stood. "Man, are you pathetic," he said as he walked away.

Delia's chair screeched across the hardwood floor. She thrust herself up and threw her napkin on the table. It landed in her plate of unfinished food as she snapped her head to face away from her father and followed her brother out of the room.

Max sought solace where he always had. In the arms of his wife. She could no longer be his wife in many ways, most ways, but she still enjoyed his touch. He made love to her and fell into an exhausted sleep.

The next morning, he brought out the old photo albums. The doc said the pictures might help jog her memory. "Remember this?" he asked, pointing to the picture of a tall thin man, a shock of black sweat-drenched hair slashed across his brow, his deep brown eyes a-smolder as he smiled ecstatically into the camera. His arm wrapped tightly around the young woman at his side, who smiled up at him with the face of an angel. Long blond curls cascaded in shining waves to the slender waist his fingers clutched. Max could imagine the feel of the soft coil touching his knuckles. Her left hand rested lightly upon his chest, the bright gold ring prominent on the third finger.

When Camilla didn't answer, he continued. "The happiest day of my life."

Then Camilla smiled and ran a tentative finger over the photo. "Yes, so happy," her voice was barely above a whisper. Her brow furrowed and she raised her gaze to his. "Who are they?"

"They're us, sweetheart. They're us." He closed the album and set it on the bedside table.

"It's time to get up. We have to go see the doctor today."

"Okay. But first I want to look at the pictures."

"We already did that."

"I want to look again."

"No. Not right now." He pulled back the covers. Her bones poked through the fabric of her pajamas. He groaned. She had wet the bed. "C'mon," he coaxed, grabbing her thin hand.

"No," she wailed. He was unprepared when her other hand walloped the side of his head, causing his ear to ring. He lost his balance and, abruptly letting go of her, fell hard onto the bed.

"Leave me alone!" she screamed, pushing him away with her feet, then kicking and flailing her arms. Getting over the shock, Max struggled to grab her arms and hold them by her sides. He used his weight to stop her legs from moving.

"Get off me!" she cried, tossing her head, trying to find purchase to bite him.

Max managed to hold her still and keep his head away from her teeth. "Shhh, shhh. It's okay." He spoke softly. "It's okay. I'm not going to hurt you. You're all right. It's all right."

She started sobbing.

"Hush now," he murmured, collecting her into his arms. "Hush."

She pushed him away. "Who are you? What are you doing here?"

At that, his tears began to flow. Wrapped in each other's arms, they sat on the urine-soaked sheets, and, together, they wept.

Later, while the nurses were dealing with his wife's toilette, for she refused to let Max bathe or dress her, the doctor delivered the bad news. "Camilla's body is shutting down. It's forgetting everything. How to aspirate. How to create white blood cells. How to pump blood. It won't be much longer now."

"Doc, I—" Max lowered his head and stared at his shoes. "I can't do it anymore." He rubbed the back of his neck. "I can't take care of her any longer."

"I understand," the doc said with the first compassion Max had heard in the man's voice. "I'll make the arrangements." He started writing in her file. "At this stage, we won't be putting her in a home. We'll be putting her in hospice." He clicked his pen closed.

So much for compassion. Upon noticing Max's stricken face, the doctor softened his professional demeanor and put a hand on Max's shoulder. "I just want you to know that . . . what you have done . . . keeping her at home all this time, and caring for her yourself . . . Well, it's just heroic. That's what it is. Heroic. And I . . . I wanted to tell you that."

Max couldn't thank him, couldn't even answer him. He pressed his lips together to keep from bawling and nodded.

Two weeks later he called the kids home.

Two days after that Camilla was dead.

They all gathered at his house after the funeral—friends, relatives, well-wishers. The house he had shared with her, the house she had so lovingly made into a home for their family, the house she would never return to again. He'd been surprised by how many people had attended the service and inurnment, then followed on to the wake.

He sat in one of the hard chairs of the formal dining table. His body feeling so heavy, he feared the spindle legs wouldn't be able to bear it and would fail and flatten beneath him. He shifted his weight, trying to sit lighter.

The buzz of conversation rose and fell around him. He let the hum hit his ears and bounce back without actually hearing a word. An occasional punctuation of laughter made the gathering sound almost like a party. Parties made Camilla nervous. People coming up to her, talking to her as if they knew her. Her, not recognizing them at all. He pushed himself up from the chair. He had to go find her and make sure she wasn't scared or agitated. He stepped to the end of the table and peered around. Then he remembered and dragging his feet returned his seat in the hard chair.

The kids went on with their lives. He expected nothing less.

He got on as best he could. Initially, he'd experienced a kind of euphoria. He was free. He could do whatever he pleased. No Camilla, Camilla, Camilla. He cleaned out her closet, filled a dozen trash bags with her clothes, threw out all her toiletries, gave away those hideous throw pillows she'd loved. He sorted through the pantry and refrigerator and removed any items that had been "hers." He only watched sports, news and the occasional western on TV.

He usually fell asleep in front of the television with an empty bottle next to him. The bourbon helped him to stop thinking. But sometimes when he was drinking, she would come to him, talk to him, accuse him.

She'd take him with her to revisit the night she'd confessed her great sin to him.

He remembered the smell of booze on her when she had walked in.

The first thing she'd said was, "Where're the kids?"

It was a good thing that she had missed saying goodbye to them earlier that day as they left for a week at church camp. He never could have hidden it otherwise. The ultimate outcome of that drunken confession.

"This all could have been avoided," he said to his wife's ghost. "I never would have hit you or shook you so hard. I wouldn't have, if you just hadn't slept with him. As long as I live, I will never understand why you had an affair with the man who had been my commanding officer, the man I looked up to more than any other on this earth. The man who was my closest friend. It is his death I regret. His death that fills me with grief and guilt. How much of my life, how much of myself I lost because of you. I hope you do go to Hell."

And thus ends the story of Max, a good man, for the most part.

Why I Wrote this Story

Thank you for reading. This story was inspired by a family member who was a true hero in his years-long efforts of looking after his sick wife. A man who rarely, if ever, faltered in this duty. His unwavering devotion and the compassionate, thoughtful attention with which he cared for his partner stirred my soul, made me wish I had someone who would love me with such intensity. My aim in writing "For the Most Part," was to pen a sort of homage. But . . . as I was typing away, I asked myself that question writers often use to spur their work forward, "What if?" The answer led me down a different path, a dark and twisted one. I take full responsibility for the turn into the shadows. It was my mind that wandered from the light into the terrors of the night.

Lost Boy of Sudan

Patricia Taylor Wells

Lost Boy of Sudan
Patricia Taylor Wells

When my neighbor Sherry asked me to come over, I didn't suspect she had more on her mind than sitting by the swimming pool and having a glass of wine. It was late September; the leaves had begun to change colors, and the temperature was mild. Sherry wasted no time with small talk.

"I wonder if you could help me out?" Sherry began. "I've agreed to host two Lost Boys in my home."

"Lost Boys?" I asked. "How old are they, and where are their parents?"

"First, let me explain. I'm talking about two boys from southern Sudan who recently came to the United States with the help of the International Rescue Committee. There were about 20,000 young boys who fled to Ethiopia following the brutal murder of their families and the destruction of their villages.

"But didn't that take place a while back?" I asked.

"Yes, it was during the civil war of 1987. Most of the boys were only six or seven years old. They were working in the fields, tending cattle when the slaughter occurred. They could hear the horrific screams of their family members and knew they had to flee. During the next few months and years, they walked more than a thousand miles to escape death or induction into the Northern Army. Those were their choices. Half of the boys died before reaching the Kakuma refugee camp in Kenya."

"I can't imagine what that would be like," I said. "Aren't these boys grown now?"

"Yes and no. The savage war had stolen the young boys' childhoods and forced them to parent themselves in a way few of us can imagine. The workers in the camp began referring to them as the Lost Boys, like the children's story of the orphaned boys led by Peter Pan in Never Land. Like Peter Pan, they had never grown up, although they were young men in their early twenties by then."

"So, what is it you want me to do?" I hoped Sherry was not suggesting that I also host a Lost Boy. My husband Robert would never agree to it, and I wasn't sure if I had what it takes to host someone.

"The boys learned English in the refugee camp but little else. The things we take for granted, such as drawing water from a faucet, flushing a toilet, or turning on a light switch, are foreign to them. One of the boys I'm hosing has been hired by Radio Shack to help receive and shelve supplies since he's more advanced in English. Since you do the neighborhood newsletter, I thought you could post an ad for the other boy. Or ask anyone you know if they could help him find work that doesn't require much skill or knowledge. His name is Peter, a common name given to many of the Lost Boys."

"I would be glad to do that. In the meantime, perhaps I could hire Peter to help me weed my flower beds. They are pretty ragged due to my neglect."

"You understand that you will have to show him everything you want him to do?" asked Sherry. "Although he worked in the fields of Sudan, he has no clue about flower beds. He might just as well mistake your roses or azaleas as a weed."

"I'll work alongside him. Send Peter over at ten o'clock tomorrow morning. I will be out front waiting for him."

"Thank you so much," said Sherry.

"Well, I can't believe you are doing this. I hope all goes well."

The following day, I went outside to determine where to start weeding. At precisely ten o'clock, I saw a tall, thin man walking up the driveway. I had not expected him to be taller than me. His skin was as dark as coal and very shiny. Peter did not smile, and he looked at me with uncertainty.

"Hello, Peter," I greeted him.

"Hello, Mrs., I am here to work."

"Please call me Patricia."

"Yes, *Pa-tri-cia.*"

"Or you can call me Pat if that is easier for you. Let's sit on the sidewalk so I can show you what to do."

Peter and I sat down with our knees bent and our legs folded beneath us. I gave him a garden spade and showed him how to pull up weeds.

"Why do you do this?" asked Peter.

"Weeds choke the garden. They rob plants of water, food, sunshine, and space. Weeds can harm the plants we eat and those we enjoy looking at."

"But why grow plants you do not eat?"

"That's a good question, Peter. But here, we like to have beautiful plants to look at."

"I ate any plant I saw when I was hungry."

"Not every plant is good to eat and can make you sick. Oh, but look, the deer have eaten some of my shrubs." I sighed upon seeing how much damage they had done to my azaleas.

Peter grew very quiet.

"Is something wrong?" I asked.

"Will the deer eat me?" Peter spoke like a child.

"Why would you think that? Of course not!'

"When the other boys in the field and I fled to escape the soldiers as they murdered our families, we had nothing but the clothes on our backs. We had little to eat, mainly berries and leaves. We sometimes ate soft mud if there was no river water to drink. Villagers along the way offered us food, which largely kept us alive. We were afraid to sleep, no matter how tired we were. Eventually, we met up with more boys who had endured the same fate. The older boys became our leaders, although most were only twelve or thirteen."

"I don't think I would have lasted very long under those conditions," I said.

"We suffered hunger and constant danger. Our biggest threats were militia gunfire and being eaten alive by lions or leopards as we ran across sub-Saharan Africa in search of safety. Often, we had to dive into the river to escape the soldiers and predators. The river, too, became a watery grave for those who couldn't swim or were attacked by crocodiles.

"I can't even imagine what your life must have been like, Peter."

There was a silence that fell over us. There was nothing I could think of to say that could erase the pain this young man would carry with him for the rest of his life. I now understood how Peter, a grown man with the innocence of a child, was afraid of encountering the deer that grazed on my garden beds.

"I try not to let my past make me afraid of things," Peter stated.

"You do not have to be afraid of the deer; they mainly eat plants. And if you came across a deer, they would flee faster than you could blink your eyes."

As Peter and I pulled weeds, I thought about how children in all societies are nurtured by their parents, family, and community and by the stories, legends, and myths passed down from generation to generation. The lessons they learn teach them values and essential skills for overcoming life's difficulties. Without these fundamental teachings, the Lost Boys relied entirely on the strongest instinct of all – survival.

Around noon, I brought out some small plates with fruit, cheese, and crackers for Peter and me. Peter especially liked the lemonade I had made. After lunch, I suggested we work on another project. Peter seemed grateful not to have to pull any more weeds.

"We are going to paint my picket fence," I said. "The color is fading and needs a touch-up."

We went to the backyard. I opened the can of bluish-green plaint and gave Peter a brush. I was sure he had never painted a fence.

"Let me show you," I said as I dipped my brush into the can. Peter watched as I painted two slats. "Now you try."

Peter carefully applied the paint on several slats. He looked at me and said, "You can go away now. I can do this."

I smiled at Peter and put down my paintbrush. I felt sure Peter would be just fine, no matter what he did in the coming months and years.

Most Lost Boys in America became U.S. citizens and graduated from college. Many returned to their former homes in Sudan, only to find that a new war had broken out.

I still think of Peter and hope he is safe wherever he may be.

Why I Wrote this Story

This story is based on my experience with a Lost Boy of Sudan. It touched my heart and opened my eyes to how we view things according to our life experiences. While I was worried about deer eating my azaleas, Peter was worried about being eaten alive by them. Most of all, this story reveals the incredible strength of survival and how we can overcome the worst of circumstances.

Goodbye, Marco
A Love Remembered

A Short Story

B Alan Bourgeois

Goodbye, Marco
A Love Remembered
B Alan Bourgeois

Dear Marco,

When I first saw you at the Escape Resort in Palm Springs, I had no idea that you would change my life forever. It was a typical sunny afternoon when I walked into the courtyard, eager to start my weekend getaway. As I approached the entrance, I saw you walking out, and for a brief moment, our eyes met. There was an instant connection, a spark that neither of us could ignore. Your smile was the brightest and most genuine I had ever seen, and it lit up my soul in a way I had never experienced before.

Your shoulder-length black curly hair framed your face perfectly, accentuating your big, beautiful smile. It was the kind of smile that made everything else fade away. I couldn't help but smile back at you, and for that brief moment, it felt like the world stood still. As I continued towards the reception, I couldn't help but glance back to watch you walk out to the parking lot. You moved with a grace and confidence that captivated me, and I found myself hoping that I would see you again during my stay.

I checked into my room and began to settle in for the weekend. The resort was new to me, but Palm Springs was not. I had visited the city a dozen times when I lived in Los Angeles thirty years ago. There was something nostalgic and comforting about being back, yet everything felt new and exciting. After unpacking, I decided to step out to the grocery store to grab some basic food items for my stay. When I returned, I took a long shower, letting the warm water wash away the stress of my journey. As I prepared to relax for the night, I couldn't shake the image of you from my mind.

The next morning, I woke up feeling refreshed and eager to explore the city. I enjoyed a simple breakfast of fruit and a caffeine drink in my room, all the while watching the people walk along the walkway from my window. I wasn't quite ready to face the world yet, so I wrapped myself in one of the resort's robes and enjoyed some people-watching from the comfort of my room. There was something exhilarating about seeing the variety of people passing by, each with their own story to tell.

As the morning progressed, I decided it was time to start my day. I showered quickly, got dressed, and set out to explore the city. The resort was perfectly situated for easy walking or bike riding to various attractions, and I spent a couple of hours getting reacquainted with Palm Springs. The city had changed in some ways, yet many of the places I remembered were still there, evoking fond memories of my younger days.

By 11 AM, I was back at the resort, ready to enjoy the warm sun by the pool. I stripped down to my birthday suit, grabbed a towel, and headed out to the courtyard. The weather was perfect, with clear blue skies and a gentle breeze. I found an open lounge chair and settled in, eager to soak up the sun and relax.

As I lay there, eyes closed and completely at ease, I heard the sound of water splashing in the pool. I opened my eyes and saw you swimming. At first, I wasn't sure if it was really you, but the curly black hair and your graceful movements were unmistakable. You stopped at the far end of the pool, turned to look at me, and smiled. My heart skipped a beat as I smiled back, feeling a mix of excitement and nervousness.

You swam towards my end of the pool, and to my surprise, you came over to the ledge closest to me and stopped. "Hello," you said in a broken Spanish accent.

"Howdy," I replied softly, trying to mask my nervousness.

"I saw you yesterday when I was heading out," you said, your eyes locked onto mine.

"Yes, I saw you too. You have a great smile," I responded, giving you my best smile in return.

"Thanks," you said, looking directly at me. "It's always a pleasure to smile at a Daddy."

Oh, he's good, I thought to myself. That was a flirt if there ever was one. I chuckled and replied, "I'm Alan, Daddy, or Sir, depending on your mood."

"Oh, I like the options," you smiled big at me. "I'm Marco."

"Howdy Marco."

"Howdy Daddy."

At that moment, I guessed you were in your mid-thirties compared to my mid-sixties. The age difference didn't bother me; in fact, I preferred the energy and enthusiasm of younger men. You seemed to embody everything I admired: confidence, kindness, and a zest for life.

"What brings you to Palm Springs?" you asked, genuinely curious.

"A little vacation time before the holidays," I replied. "You?"

"The same."

"Where are you from?"

You smiled and asked, "Now or before I came to America?"

"Let's start with now," I said, smiling.

"Phoenix," you responded. "I have lived there for ten years and come to Palm Springs every year before the holidays."

"Nice. Then you must know the city very well by now," I said, hoping you might offer to show me around.

"Yes, I can tell you where to go and what to see if you like."

"That would be great," I smiled sheepishly, hoping that would be the response you gave me.

You pulled yourself out of the water in front of me, allowing me to see your toned muscles at work. Standing there before me, you looked even more impressive, with a slight amount of hair between your chest muscles and a small trail from your navel down to your groin. It was clear that you took care of yourself, and I admired that.

We continued talking, sharing stories about our lives and experiences. You told me about your job in Phoenix, your family, and your love for traveling. I shared my own stories, my experiences, and my hopes for the future. We talked for hours, and it felt like we had known each other forever. There was an undeniable connection between us, one that I hadn't felt in a long time.

That evening, we had dinner together and went to one of the local bars. We danced, laughed, and enjoyed each other's company. It was a night filled with joy and newfound companionship. By the end of the night, we found ourselves back in my room, where we continued to talk and learn more about each other. We shared our dreams, our fears, and our goals. Your passion for life was infectious, and I found myself opening up to you in ways I hadn't with anyone else in a very long time.

The next morning, we woke up early and decided to spend the day exploring Palm Springs together. We walked around the town, visited the mountain sky shuttle, and hiked for a couple of hours on the trails. The entire day was filled with laughter, deep conversations, and moments of quiet reflection. You showed me parts of the city I hadn't seen before and introduced me to local spots that had become your favorites over the years.

As the sun began to set, we returned to the resort for dinner. You suggested a local restaurant that you loved, and it didn't disappoint. The food was excellent, but the company was even better. We talked about everything and nothing, enjoying each other's presence and the growing bond between us.

After dinner, we returned to the resort. You walked me to my door, and before I could open it, you leaned in and kissed me softly. It was a sweet, tender moment that took my breath away. We spent the rest of the evening in my room, talking and sharing more about our lives. The connection between us deepened, and I felt a sense of peace and happiness that I hadn't felt in years.

The next morning, we woke up early, knowing it was our last day together before we had to head back to our respective homes. We agreed to meet at the airport to say goodbye, and the thought of leaving you made my heart ache.

At the airport, we found a quiet spot and hugged each other tightly. We had agreed to meet up again in a couple of months, and the promise of seeing you again gave me hope. As we stood there, I felt a tear welling up in my eye, and I knew you could see it. Before I could wipe it away, you kissed my eye and whispered, "I think I am in love."

I squeezed you hard and said, "So am I." You squeezed me back with the same intensity.

Then, we heard your flight being called to board. We pulled apart, tears of joy and sadness on our faces. You turned and walked towards your gate, looking back one last time to send me a kiss through the air. I was in trouble. I had no choice but to let the tears roll down my cheeks.

I was a sap, and I didn't care. I turned to my gate, wiped the tears away, and walked towards it. I grabbed my phone and took a picture of my wet face and sent it to you. I wrote, "It's your fault I look like a mess. But thank you for being the reason for it." I hit send and went to sit down.

A couple of minutes later, you texted back, "I hope to do it again real soon. Love, Marco."

I smiled and put the phone away. My flight was uneventful, and as usual, I was home that night, back in my bed. Before I fell asleep, I read a text from you saying you made it back to Phoenix okay and would text me the next day to start talking about our next meet-up.

I sent you a kiss emoji and wrote, "I can't wait."

I didn't hear from you the next day as expected, but I wasn't too worried. You mentioned you would be busy catching up on work. However, by mid-day Wednesday, I received a text from your phone. It read, "This is Marcy, Marco's sister. I have some bad news for you. Marco was hit by a car while on a run and died yesterday."

I was frozen. I kept reading it over and over before I responded. "I'm sorry, is this a cruel joke?" I replied.

"No, I am sorry it is not. The funeral will be held on Friday at…"

I dropped the phone, realizing that the man I had begun to fall in love with was gone in an instant. I curled up into a ball and cried my heart out.

I woke up in the same spot the next morning, unable to believe what had happened. I picked up my phone to check the time and saw more messages from your number.

"He told me when he got home that he met you and how he was feeling about you."

"I know this must be painful for you, as it is for us. Just know that in the short time he knew you, he had fallen in love with you."

I began to cry once more. I too had fallen in love with you. As quickly as I met you, I now had to say goodbye.

I opened my photo app and scrolled through the few pictures I had of us together. One was of us hiking, another at dinner on Saturday night, one of us dancing, and the last one was of you standing at the door before you left to go home.

I called in sick to work and stayed home. I had to figure out a way to say goodbye to you. I wasn't going to the funeral. I didn't know anyone, and I felt it wouldn't be appropriate.

So, I chose to write you this letter recapping that short weekend we meet and fell in love.

"I began to fall in love with you by the end of the first day. While I knew I should let you be on your own to enjoy your vacation, I just could not let you go. You made me happy in ways I can never explain. I felt alive, loved, and happy.

"To learn how fast I lost you has torn me apart. I was so looking forward to seeing you again and to learn more about you over the days and months to come.

"I know that I was right to fall in love with you. As my heart

53

Goodbye, Marco

breaks knowing it is not meant to be anymore, I want you to know that you were loved, and I will always cherish you.

"I pray to God, He takes care of you now. Until I can see you again, may I remain open to the love that you have shown me until my dying days.

"With all my love, Goodbye Marco.

"Love, Alan"

I folded up the letter and lit it on fire. As it began to burn, I put it down on a small plate and watched it disintegrate into ashes. I closed my eyes and silently prayed for you to receive it above and to feel the love I sent with it.

I then went to bed and cried myself to sleep.

The end.

Why I Wrote This Story

During my years of traveling around the world, I met many people in a variety of ways. As a gay man, I often traveled alone, which gave me the freedom to meet other men in exotic cities. Some of these encounters turned into holiday romances that ended when I boarded the plane home, while others were more difficult to leave behind. Each time, it was a challenge to find a way to close those chapters in my heart and return to my normal life. In one particular case, I chose to write a love letter with a tragic ending, allowing me to find closure and move on.

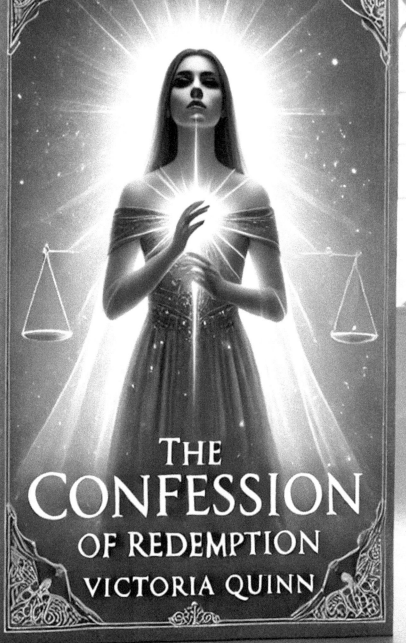

THE
CONFESSION
OF REDEMPTION
VICTORIA QUINN

The Confession of Redemption
Victoria Quinn

I want to share a *confession* with you. I am going through a painful, emotional, and unforgiving betrayal of infidelity in my marriage that caused me to react with anger. Not just any type of anger, but anger lingering for a couple of years. I'm surprised I lasted this long without having a nervous breakdown, but by the Grace of God, I did not. Being a leader in the church, you would think I would know better not to allow myself to hold on to the hurt for so long, but I'm human. No one expects a leader in the church to be perfect, but they expect their personal life to be. As a believer, I vowed to God to serve Him wholeheartedly and forgive others when they betray your trust. But unforgiveness feels unfair and hard to do when you're beyond brokenness. How do you come back from your heart being torn apart, your soul crushed, and your trust destroyed? The Lord says in His Holy word that He will shut the mouths of wolves, but what if the wolf that He is shutting up is you?

The enemy will try to use *you* against *you*. I was at my lowest, and the enemy took advantage of my emotions. I didn't know how to filter out the anger that tormented me daily until one day, when I least expected it, I met this Man. He was the perfect gentleman, so kind, compassionate, comforting, and sensitive to my feelings and needs, something I wasn't used to. He left an impression that warmed my heart. At that moment, I felt an overwhelming sense of joy that put a smile on my face. It was an amazing feeling because He was like no other man I ever met. I know it may sound odd, but this is my *confession*.

I crossed paths with this Man on several occasions. There was something about this Man that made me want to get to know Him, so I asked Him out on a date. One date led to another date, and then another. We would meet more often than usual. I really liked this Guy! We would tour the city, take long walks in the park, listen to gospel music and sing together, or have lunch in a private spot and just talk. My heart skips a beat every time I see Him. No one would understand the deep love I have for this Man. He would send birds to serenade me outside my bedroom window every morning. He would shine a light upon my face when I walked outside my door. He would bring me flowers that bloom in the spring to remind me of His love for me. He promised that He would be there for me if I ever needed Him. Some may say that it sounds like a fairy tale, but whether you believe it or not, this is my *confession*.

I cleared my schedule so I could spend more one-on-one time with Him. I was shocked that He knew everything about me, including my ugly past, but He didn't care. He wanted to spend time with me anyway. I love who I am when I'm with Him. He had a great sense of humor and made me laugh when I was sad. I would pass up opportunities to hang out with family and friends just to be with Him. This may sound silly, but this is my *confession*.

When I lay on my pillow at night, I think of Him. His perfect love made my heart want to live again. I look forward to waking up every morning before my alarm goes off, excited to have a cup of coffee with Him, and read the Holy Bible together. He explained things I didn't understand like a teacher would with a student. The more I read, the more I was willing to learn. He was a great and wise teacher. He spoke about His Father and how His Father taught Him as He grew up. I learned a lot from Him. He changed everything about me, from the way I speak, and the way I treat people to the way I treat myself. No matter where I went, He was there. I was never alone. I fell in love with this Man, and I knew He felt the same about me. I have never met anyone like Him. He was different. I was comfortable enough to share everything with Him, from my anger, confusion, frustration, and hurt of betrayal. He listened without judging me. "Please pray for me." Those were the words I whispered from a place of my brokenness. I cried out to Him and said, "How many times does the Lord expect me to forgive? When is enough, enough?"

He held my hand with compassion and mercy. It's like He knew how I felt. My tears were His tears. My pain was His pain. He comforted me and counseled me. Sometimes, it's not pride that's holding you back, it's the hurt and bitterness that shattered your heart into pieces. I realized that the only person who can stop me from my deliverance…is me.

Instead of giving me a lecture, He gave me hope, strength, encouragement, and promises to never leave me. I feel protected when I'm in His presence. It was then I realized that I love Him more than I love my husband, my children, and myself. I know that sounds over the top, but this is my *confession*.

Just when I thought I had it all together, my past caught up with me, and I ended up in court. When I called on Him to represent me, He didn't hesitate and came to my rescue. As I looked around the courtroom, I started having regrets. I never imagined that my hurt from the past would dictate my emotions to end up here in court before the Throne of God for judgment. As I sat next to the Man I loved, I glanced around the courtroom, and there he was, the Accuser, pleading his charges against me with his lies. This is what he said to the court, "The offense cannot be ignored or overlooked. This woman is guilty of unforgiveness, resentment, bitterness, and anger. She should not be called to serve as a leader in Your Kingdom." His words were vicious, full of poison. It was like he wanted me to curse God, surrender, and accept defeat.

I made eye contact briefly with my Accuser, and he smirked at me as he sat down.

The Man I loved stood up and said in my defense, "We cannot be overcomers without trouble to overcome. It is true that bad things happen to good people, but Heavenly Father, You use those bad things of the world to equip believers for a deeper ministry. Your servant is a woman who answered the *call* to serve in Your Kingdom. She has been falsely accused of unforgiveness, bitterness, and anger. I will prove without a reasonable doubt that not only is she capable of forgiveness, but she will overcome her brokenness and be redeemed into newness. The Accuser is threatened and intimated by Your servant's strong faith and is out to steal her identity and ruin her position in the church. I will prove that the Accuser is a liar and deceiver trying to take what is not his. We are asking that You turn a deaf ear to the lies that the Accuser has presented in this courtroom."

I stared at the Man I love in awe. His defense amazed me. He knew it was tough for me back then because of the wounds left on my broken heart. As I reflect on those times of darkness, I faced the ultimate betrayal in my marriage more than once, and unforgiveness was truly against me. I was guilty. There are no words to describe the betrayal, anger, or disappointment I felt back then. Betrayal changes things, and it can change you if you allow it to.

The Confession of Redemption

My faith was on trial. My faith had to outlast the pain of the past, outlast the troubles of the past, outlast the heartache, sorrow, and misery of the past. I fasted through the suffering, and I prayed on my knees through the suffering. I was wrestling with God for my freedom, and I was not letting Him go until He helped me break free and redeem me. I was determined to get back the life that was stolen from me, but the battle in the courtroom was fierce, and the Accuser was after my soul, to destroy my life and my future.

Through the trial, I listened as the Man I loved defended me in my darkest hour when there was no hope. He filled me with His Spirit and His Peace by His actions and His words. It appeared He wasn't surprised by the schemes of the Accuser. This was not His first court appearance. He rescued me from myself, from being someone He did not *call* me to be. He intervened on my behalf. I was convinced that this was not going to beat me; the troubled waters will not drown me because He is my anchor. The scorching fire will not burn me because He is protecting me from the flames. The violent wind can't blow me away because my faith is built on The Rock, and His strength will be my strength to get me through the storm.

"Heavenly Father," my Redeemer continued, "there's no truth to what the Accuser is charging Your servant of, and we call for the dismissal of all charges against her and that Your servant be redeemed to her rightful place to continue her journey in God's Kingdom."

After an hour of deliberation, I walked out of that courtroom with my freedom. I looked like a different person of newness, a forgiving person with a new beginning, and a fresh anointing. Letting go of the betrayal was the best thing for me. I was no longer the person the deceiver portrayed me to be. The old me was gone. I am redeemed. This is my *confession of redemption*.

I smiled at the Man I loved and said, "Thank you, Lord."

Jesus returned the smile. "Your sins are paid in *full*, now go and walk in your purpose."

"See you tomorrow," I told Him.

He nodded in agreement and then returned to the courtroom to defend another believer.

Why I Wrote this Story

Before I wrote this short inspirational story, I was hesitant to share it. I felt it was embarrassing to allow myself to be vulnerable about my personal life, especially with me being a leader in the church. Nevertheless, I noticed other women and even men in and out of the church who were going through the same betrayal of infidelity. It was then I was inspired to share how I got through it and walked away afterward stronger with no more pain, sorrow, or heartache.

2 Corinthians 1:3-4 (NIV) says, "Praise be to the God and Father of our Lord Jesus Christ, the Father of compassion and the God of all comfort, who comforts us in all our troubles, so that we can comfort those in any trouble with the comfort we ourselves receive from God." A brief version of my inspirational story will be featured in the September 2024 issue of BWA (Black Women Author) Magazine.

Life After...
Roxanne Gail Hodge

Life After …
Roxanne Gail Hodge

My daughter just left the room. It's over. The love of my life for over 60 years is now in the presence of Jesus, celebrating and dancing with the angels. I'm good with that. It had been years, or had it just been months? Anyway, she hasn't been good with life for a long time. Oh, she tried and still showed her sense of humor now and then, but I could tell she was just tired. I think the unknown and her concern for the ones she would leave behind kept her going as long as she did.

Right now, I'm going to go back to sleep and relax. There will no longer be a need to get up early and get ready to spend the day keeping vigil at the hospital. My daughter is here to decide the next steps, and she assures me the family is here to help me through these days.

* * *

I woke up this morning without my love. I was disoriented momentarily and wondered if she had gotten up before me. Then I remembered, with a fleetingly sharp pain in my chest, that she would no longer be by my side when I was asleep or awake. The strangest feeling came right after the pain, which was relief. Of course, I will never admit to feeling relief to anyone because that makes me sound cruel and hardhearted. The immediate problem is to figure out how other people expect me to act and perform so I won't disappoint anyone.

Breakfast is over. It wasn't breakfast as usual because my daughter sat with me the entire time I ate. We didn't talk much. I got the feeling she wasn't sure what to say. I quit knowing what to say years ago unless I had a question about something specific. My wife and I didn't say much in the last few years. Oh, we would comment about the weather or the wind, maybe about the squirrels and birds playing outside our window. Mostly, we just sat together and ate. I don't know what I thought about this remarkable woman I've been with for years. Perhaps I didn't think anything.

I'm ready for bed, yet when I see the clock, I realize it's much too early. Maybe it doesn't matter because normal life is gone. I can set a new normal. My love was one to stay up late, so I accommodated as I could. She liked to laze around in bed after waking up, and I also accommodated that. I did it because I liked being by her side. Now, I can go to bed early, get up early, jump out of bed, and begin the day. I decided to get my PJs on. I'm sure my daughter will be in any moment to bring me my bedtime pills. She'll also bring in that dreaded hot chocolate I tolerate to humor her. I wonder if I can refuse the nightly ritual after a while. She means well. All these thoughts about the future cycle through my mind, and I prepare for bed.

* * *

There were so many people in and out of the house today. My daughter told me everything she did or would do and acted like I had a say. She tries to, bless her heart, but what she doesn't know is that most of the time, I don't care. She is more than capable of doing whatever needs to be done. I let her keep me updated because even though she makes good decisions, I can change the trajectory if I don't agree or like the way it's going. The relationship works. I wonder how it will work now. My mate was more needy and required more attention to keep going every day. Poor daughter, she tried to get something out of her mother that I don't think was there anymore. Sometimes, it's okay to let go of what has always been and make room for the "what is now." She'll learn. Tomorrow, there will be more people and more food. I think I've eaten more in the last two days than I have in two months.

* * *

I couldn't sleep last night and was up way before anyone. I decided to work on my puzzle. About an hour after I was up, my daughter came and talked to me. She said it was too early to be up (as if I needed to be told) and to see if I could get a couple more hours. She left and, I'm sure, went back to bed herself. I was already dressed, so after doing a little more on my puzzle, I sat in my recliner and closed my eyes. When I woke up, I was surprised by how long I had slept in my chair. More food, more people. Yet when there isn't anyone around, I can't seem to sit still. I wander around my rooms, then go into the main house, and whoever sees me asks if I need something. My answer is always "no." I'm fine, but I want to say, "No, I'm not alright! I just lost my wife, whom I've known for more than 60 years, and now, at my age, I'm supposed to figure out what life is going to look like without her!" The honest answer will make everyone sad, so I will smile and tell them everything is fine.

* * *

I slept much better last night. We went to one of the grandkid's houses, looked at pictures, reminisced about some, and planned the services. Everything was muted because of the thick fog that had settled over me. The good thing about all that is that my feelings have also been muted, so I can make it through the day relatively sanely. No one talks about being sad or how much they miss "her." I don't know if that is a good thing or a bad thing. Sometimes, I think they want to get her services over so it can just be over. I can't get angry about that, though, because underneath all of my thoughts, that is what I think also. I want to be over missing her; I want to be over getting used to life alone; I want to be there already. Maybe I want to join her also. That thought is there, but so far, I am just bobbing around it, not getting a foothold in my desires. I'm not going to bed early. That helps me sleep better later.

* * *

There was lots of shopping and discussions about what to wear at the service. My daughter came in to discuss my options and devise a plan. That will be tomorrow. I think I'm taking a shower this afternoon, so I don't have to take one in the morning. It's not easy to decide where I want to eat. I always have a choice in what I eat, but I don't always like to eat alone. The thing is, even if I eat in the dining area, I'm still eating by myself. No one seems to have time to sit and spend most of the evening with me. I wonder if they know I miss that. The pastors and the funeral home people reviewed everything that would happen tomorrow.

Life After …

We won't have the usual family in cars and all of that. It is a memorial service, not a funeral, and there won't be a graveside service right now. I've been told many relatives are coming, and some surprised me. I think it might be nice to see them. We are supposed to have a houseful after the service.

* * *

I woke up before anyone else. I didn't get up because it was too early. This is the day we have planned for over the last week. People have been discussing what to wear and trying to figure out the appropriate clothing, but my love wouldn't care. Maybe they obsess over those things because it keeps their minds occupied and free from sadness. I was dressed pretty early with nothing to do. Thankfully it was time to go before I got too restless. Once we were at the funeral home there were people to talk to. Someone was always coming up to me and taking time to chat about things for a while. I don't think I will ever remember what the two pastors said about my partner of over 60 years, but what can they say that I don't already know? Her life was my life. I guess I let my mind wander back through our lives because, before long, everyone had been standing up and getting ready to leave. Once again, I stood around with many people who came up and talked with me. I'm not sure I liked that much attention, but at least it kept me occupied. When we got to the house, there were massive amounts of food and more people than should be allowed. Everyone ate and ate and ate some more. I was sitting at the table where they put all of the children, so I guess I know my place! It was sweet because my oldest granddaughter … my only granddaughter, stayed by my side most of the day. She was highly attentive. After I finally retired to my room, one of my great-grandsons came and watched a show with me. He didn't talk much; he sat in the chair beside mine. Children seem to know when it is okay to be quiet. It was a long day. I plan to sleep long and hard because tomorrow is the first day of the rest of my life after saying goodbye to my wife.

* * *

I got up this morning, and the world was gray. I don't know if it really was or if my soul only saw gray. I dressed in my most comfortable clothes, walked right by my unmade bed, and went to breakfast. I didn't feel like making my bed, and I didn't feel like looking decent. I sat down and read the notes my daughter likes to write to tell me what to expect that day. The note told me I was going to get my blood drawn, so I couldn't stay comfortable and be in my room and stay sad. Right after breakfast, I changed clothes into something more appropriate for going out. I made my bed. When I got to the other side, I put the pillow down and remembered how picky my dear was about the position of the pillow. I readjusted it several times so she would be pleased. I stood up, looked at the bed for a minute, and realized she didn't care about those pillows. It's when the longing overwhelmed me. I didn't like that feeling, so I decided to leave my room and do something.

I will walk. The family will take me with them on their yearly trip to the mountains, so I will get ready for the trip. I decided not to do what I did yesterday when I stayed in my room. I will make a point to get out and do things.

Life is not going to be the same. I am sad, but I am surrounded by people who care about me, and I don't have to figure out the new. I will remember to let those around me know when I don't like what they decide for me. Mostly, my daughter is respectful and not presumptuous in the decisions she makes concerning me.

I realize this is my life now, and I go to my recliner and sit.

Why I Wrote this Story

I became a live-in caregiver in November 2022, assisting an only child in caring for her parents. Her mother passed on in January of 2023. I observed the interactions and reactions of all parties involved ready to assist in any manner needed. I knew my life would look different now that she was gone. As I watched people come and go, my heart went out to this gentleman under my care. I tried to imagine what might be going on in his mind as he, too, faced a different life and wrote this story in his honor. Herbert Dale Lewis, at 92, is a remarkable man and lives life to the fullest. His smile lights up a room, and I am grateful to have been welcomed into his equally remarkable family.

Feels Like

Cynthia Darwin

Feels Like
Cynthia Darwin

Marilyn stood in front of the bathroom mirror and added still one more layer of lipstick. She had been advised that particular shade of red would stand out better for her audience, although she generally preferred a more natural look. It was just about time to face them again and her heartbeat went up a click or two.

It wasn't supposed to be this way, she thought to herself. In the beginning it was exciting, a dream come true. A chance to show off her knowledge and expertise. A Cinderella career as a scientist.

That was before people found out she was really good at numbers. Before she gathered a following that came to believe everything she said. Before she became the soothsayer they all counted on to tell them what lay in their future, both for minute-by-minute choices as well as life changing decisions.

At first it was just those small decisions they wanted her to weigh in on. Like, should they go to Vegas this weekend. Marilyn would know, they said. Or even higher stake decisions, like should I buy a house in this town?

I went to school for this, Marilyn thought to herself wryly. Top of her class in Statistics, a science she came to understand both theoretically and instinctively. She was able to hone calculations to a razor edge and had a 95% probability of being correct.

Friday night at college was game time for Marilyn and her academic cohorts. They would gather over beer and pizza with calculators and laptops, perusing the weekly events and feeling the climate of the times. Each running his or her favorite model, they would write out their predictions for the weekend on a folded piece of paper.

Monday morning when the different markets opened they would check the news to see if any of their predictions had played out correctly.

Monday evening the person whose educated guess was farthest from the truth would cook dinner for the others. Marilyn rarely had to cook, which was good since her idea of hosting usually involved heating up take-out.

She missed those days the most. She enjoyed the excitement of being "most right", and knew the weekly competitions sharpened her skills. Overall, it was a game of expertise with a little throw of the dice built in. Sometimes you hit it dead center, but sometimes you could be way off the mark.

It didn't matter back then. It was a game.

Then it became a job. And her followers' livelihoods, sometimes their lives, depended on her accuracy.

She wanted to tell them that it's still always a guessing game. A recipe that starts with numbers, seasoned with a little experience and a dash of intuition sprinkled in, and the answers would spit out.

"I'm good," she wanted to say out loud, "but I'm not God."

These days Marilyn was beginning to think she might have been content with a research career in her field, maybe one that blew her to the far corners, a career where she could play around with numbers that would somehow save the world. No pressure, there.

But she had chosen this path. Or it chose her. And the pressure was high.

She was pretty, they told her. Television was her destiny. They would set her up and give her money. Who could turn that down? All she had to do is smile.

And be right.

And wear red lipstick. And a short skirt.

It was science, yes, but mostly infotainment.

So she dressed the part, put on the red lipstick, cinched in the mid-thigh dress and smiled. One good call followed another until the number of her good projections accumulated into a daily pattern that people relied on.

Now people are no longer content to just see her projections on a screen. They want to watch her in person every hour, often accompanied by icons and numbers that swirl and repeat patterns in the background.

Although Marilyn still concentrated on percentages and indexes, the people wanted a forecast of the truth, and they were basing their lives on her words. Now followers have her predictions on an app, and they check their phones and computers hourly to see if her guesses are accurate. It had become much more demanding, this guessing game.

And then there is Abraham, her first. Her first computer lab partner. If Marilyn didn't win the Friday night predictions, Abraham usually did.

Her first stay-over. Her first husband. She hoped the only one.

She loved his brain, his runner's body and his sunny disposition. Mostly she loved the way he pushed her on all fronts and still was able to mend an argument with a breezy kiss on the cheek.

When she first began making her predictions on a few public service radio stations, he was amused. Not a lot of damage to be done there, he would say laughingly, so just throw a dart at it. Despite that somewhat cavalier take on her career, he was also the first to defend her when a radio co-host once introduced Marilyn by saying, "Next, we hear from the lady who reads tea leaves."

Abraham rained insults on the guy, insisting he retract the statement and publicly defend Marilyn's scientific purity.

Tea Leaves. That was just one of the ways she had been introduced. "The woman who is going to ruin your day" was another, along with "our own Wheel of Fortune Teller"

Abraham had sustained her through those times. Meanwhile, her followers grew.

It was the TV thing that caused her relationship with Abe to change directions, get a little chillier.

They were out on the patio, enjoying a crisp Chardonay on an unseasonably warm evening, when the phone rang. A local television producer asked for Marilyn. His offer was simple. Come in for an audition, and if the focus group likes it, we want you on prime time.

"Did he ask for your resume? Your credentials. Your track record?" asked Abe.

"No," answered Marilyn. "Just come in for an audition."

Abe had been upset. "They just care what you look like? Not what comes out of your mouth? Not your success rate on predictions? You're a scientist, a statistician, not a Barbie doll."

"Well, I'm sure they want most of my predictions to be right," Marilyn had answered. "I'm sure I can do that."

"And if you don't? Can they live with the pretty girl being

wrong? Then what?"

"Have some faith, Abe. You are a financial analyst. You analyze past data. I use data to make projections, make predictions. Yes, it's science, but sometimes there's a little magic to it."

Abe sat stunned. "Did you just say Magic?"

"Well, yes. Not magic, per se, but people expect a little unpredictability in what I do, don't you think? Maybe that's why they tune in? For some excitement, to see if what I say actually happens."

"They tune in for answers! Marilyn, have you lost your mind? "

"Well, I was the one who was mostly right in college, remember, and we all used the same data. So maybe there is a special sense I have for, I don't know, just filling in the blanks? That will help."

Abe just shook his head. "Unbelievable"

The audition had gone well with the focus group, although they did recommend a darker shade of lipstick, more makeup and a shorter skirt. A station in a larger market picked up her feed and streamed her ever-changing predictions to an even larger audience.

Now she was nationally recognized just as Marilyn. Everyone knew who you were talking about.

"Want to know what's happening tomorrow? Check Marilyn's app. She's always right."

Well, maybe almost always right, Marilyn thought.

She and Abe had drifted apart emotionally, a dry spell, a far cry from their normally steamy romance. Was it professional jealousy or personal differences?

"Am I just the back-up plan?" he said. "You seem married to this business."

"That's not fair. I just have to spend a lot more time with the data. I'm getting pressure from higher up all the time. Pressure to be right every time. Sometimes it turns my brain into spaghetti."

"I don't know, it seems like you're not using the data like you used to or like you should. I heard you use the phrase 'feels like' on the air a few times."

"Oh, come on. That's still a phrase we use to describe scientific data, just with a little personality."

"I don't use it. Why don't you just go ahead and say that you feel it in your bones?" Abe argued. "And where was that magic thing last month when you missed on your prediction in Louisiana? A lot of people are without homes now down there. Wonder what they feel like? I'm just trying to protect you by suggesting you stay with the science."

"Don't you think I worry about that every day? I thought I could, but I just can't be right every time. It's still the same guessing game it always was," she answered, trying to keep the tears back. "I just don't always know. Nobody knows everything that's going to happen. Sometimes I do have to use a little intuition."

"Well, if I were you, I'd stick to the data. It doesn't lie. And it doesn't cost you your job."

Tonight the stakes were as high as they had ever been. Marilyn straightened her off- the -shoulder blouse and took her seat in front of the camera. Off screen, the anchor introduced her.

"One of the last hurricanes of the season is parked over Cuba outside the Gulf of Mexico, maybe a Category 2? Here's Marilyn, our respected meteorologist. She's about to let you know which direction you need to go to be safe. Marilyn? A lot of people depend on what you have to say. Do they need to hunker down in Texas? Where's this Sandy going?"

Away, she thought about saying. I just wish it would go away. But here goes.

Marilyn smiled at the camera, hiding her anxiety. Data or intuition? She decided and took a deep breath before announcing.

"Most models show the storm landing in the Bahamas later today, then turning north to hit a few southern coastal states before diminishing. But to me, it feels like Sandy is going to New Jersey."

Hurricane Sandy became the largest Atlantic hurricane on record that year. A Category 3 when it made landfall in Cuba, Sandy became a Category 1-equivalent extratropical cyclone that travelled up the Eastern US Coast. The storm then took an unexpected left hook and moved ashore in New Jersey, causing 158 deaths in the US and damages in excess of $65 billion. In the aftermath of the storm, meteorologists revised prediction tools and terminology in anticipation of similar weather events.

Why I Wrote This Story
Our community west of Houston took an unexpected, direct hit from Hurricane Beryl this July. Nobody had been particularly

Feels Like

worried because this Category 5 Atlantic storm was supposed to be "just" a tropical storm, "maybe a Cat 1" in places, by the time it came our way. As we sat having our breakfast coffee, the power went out and large Texas pecan trees came out of the ground by their roots, falling in front of the window with one loud crack after the other. Eight trees all together. "Didn't feel like a Cat 1" was heard more and more often as we cleared up the war-torn messes on our properties. The short story came from a pondering as to how dependent we have become on precise forecasts from our many weather outlets. As the story came together, I began "sprinkling" it with weather words. Go back and see how many you can find. The main character in "Feels Like" will join other women in an anthology of short stories to be launched in 2025 as part of the Cynthia Darwin – Storyteller website.

Click, Click

Donna Joppie

Click, Click
Donna Joppie

If we had met a year ago, I'm confident you would have considered me a sane, level-headed person. But after these last few years, I'm not sure I will ever be that again.

With that disclaimer out of the way, let me introduce myself. My name is Mark Leonard. I'm a thirty-year-old photojournalist. Not one that jumps out of helicopters in war zones or chases wildlife through Africa. I'm not that brave. My specialty is coffee table books. Don't laugh. I make a decent living telling stories with my photographs.

I've produced seven books to date. Well, not exactly. To my editor's dismay, book seven is still a work in progress. But a few books have been so popular they went into reprint. Like every writer, I live on advances and royalties.

I love everything about what I do, except for one. My publisher insists he knows what sells and decides the topics of my books. J.P. is a publishing genius but can also be stubborn as hell. However, I do what he says and have put all of my ideas on hold except for the one I've been secretly researching for years.

It's a history of New York City's 8th Street. I know what you're thinking. What's so special about 8th Street? Well, it's the cultural mecca of art, publishing, fashion, and other forms of creativity.

I've been collecting black and white photos for over three years, spanning more than a century. I've visited hundreds of resale shops and collectors' warehouses, rifling through decade after decade of people's lives and memories, looking for photos taken in that section of the city. The earliest I found were melainotypes, more commonly known as tintype reprints from the 1800s. Around 1888, Kodak handheld cameras and film were created. Then came digital cameras and computers. But research on my laptop isn't nearly as gratifying as finding a forgotten, sepia-tinted, dog-eared photograph in a dusty old shop. I have collected five overstuffed shoeboxes of photos marking the street's evolution over the years, and I'll keep doing it until this book is done.

Are you with me so far? I hope so because this is where it gets interesting. . . no, it's downright bizarre.

Late one evening, I was reeling from an earlier conversation with my editor that ended in a heated discussion. Don't get me wrong, Gwen is great, but she apparently didn't accept my explanation of depleted creative energy for the delay of my project and hung up on me. Her lack of understanding made it clear she and my publisher were running out of patience, so I spent the next three hours at my computer, trying to put meaningful words to my images, but all I came up with was garbage.

Sulking, I took the first shoebox of my photo collection from the shelf in my closet, grabbed a glass and bottle of scotch from my kitchen, and went to the living room. I poured myself a stiff drink and drank it as I paced around the room to calm down. When that didn't work, I refilled my glass and took several more drinks before going to the sofa, placing the box on my lap, and removing a handful of photos.

Somewhere near the end of my box, I must have dozed off because the sound of my glass hitting the floor jarred me awake. I jumped to my feet, dropping the box and scattering photos everywhere.

"No!" I shouted, fearing some prints had fallen into the liquid. I picked up those near the liquor first and then started gathering the others. As I was returning them to the box, one photo caught my eye. I stood gazing at it for a time before taking it and the box of pictures to my worktable. I put the picture under my work lamp and studied it.

I knew I had seen a photo of this beautiful girl's face before, but I couldn't recall where. I turned the picture over, hoping to find a name written on the back, as was common in early eras, but all I saw was a photographer's stamp and the date of September 3rd, 1903. I placed the 1903 photo at the top of my table and got to work. I went through every photo in that first shoebox, and when I didn't find her, I got the rest of my collection from the closet, carried them to my worktable, and went through them one by one.

I'm not sure how far I got before I found her again. As I looked at the second photo, I realized it was taken in almost the same location as the first, but much earlier. I turned the photo over and saw it marked September 5th, 1883. I laid it next to the other image, located my magnifier glass, and carefully scanned the girls' faces. Both women looked to be in their mid-twenties, but I could swear they were the same girl. But how was that possible? These photos were taken twenty years apart. I was thoroughly confused but invested in solving this, so I kept digging through every shoebox.

It was almost noon the following day when I finished. In my hands were seven photos of the same girl taken on 8th Street within the first ten days of September, but each was dated twenty years apart. Except for the girl, everything else had changed. The clothing, the city's skyline, horse drawn carriages, and Model A automobiles were followed by various models of cars. Yes, the first images were old and somewhat grainy, and I even considered the possibility the photographer stamped the date wrong, but definitely not every one of them.

I can't tell you how many hours I spent studying those photos and knew every inch of her face better than my own. It sounds crazy, but something in me said to find her. The last picture of her was dated September 7th, 2003, exactly twenty years ago. I opened the calendar on my phone and saw today was July 6th. This meant I had until September 10th to find her or possibly be forced to wait another twenty years.

Questions bombarded my brain. How was I going to find a girl in the next few months who may or may not even exist without people thinking I was crazy? That's when an idea struck me.

I gathered the photos and turned them over, hoping to find the names of the person who took them. I didn't bother with the earlier ones because those people had to be long dead. But I was thrilled to see the last three had the photographers' names. I knew finding the person who took the 1963 photo was a stretch, so I focused on the last two. If this failed, I didn't know where else to look.

I scanned all seven images, sent them to my tablet, and then googled the name of the last photographer. Harry Summerfield Photography was no longer in business, so I started looking for a home address. The information I found was old, so I tried not to get too excited as I drove to the location in the Bronx.

I parked in front of the modest brick home on Washington Avenue, took my tablet to the door, and rang the bell. When the door opened, I could hear what sounded like a game show on the television. A gray-haired woman looking to be in her late sixties or early seventies stood in the doorway.

"Can I help you, young man?"

"I hope so. My name is Mark Leonard. I'm a photojournalist working on a story."

"That's nice, but what does that have to do with me?"

"Actually, I'm here to see Mr. Summerfield. Is he available?"

"Harry died four years ago."

My heart sank. "Oh, I'm so sorry. Thank you for your time." I started to leave but stopped. "Mrs. Summerfield, if you don't mind, may I ask you a few questions?"

"You can ask, but I may not have the answers."

I opened my tablet, scrolled to the photo Summerfield had taken, and handed it to her. "I know it was long ago, but do you recall anything about this photo? It's one of your husband's."

She looked down at it, then shoved the tablet back to me. "I don't want to talk about her," and reached for the door.

I pushed against it with my hand. "Please, Mrs. Summerfield. This is important. What can you tell me about the young woman in the photo?"

She crossed her arms and glared at me. "I can see she's gotten to you, too."

I was in shock. "Are you saying you know her?"

"That woman wrecked my life. My Harry was never the same after he took that picture."

"What do you mean?"

"Harry was obsessed with her. Nothing mattered to him but her. We lost our business, our car, and almost our home. He was so heartsick for her that it made him physically sick. I spent the rest of his life caring for him." She reached out and took my hand. "Come. There's something you need to see."

I followed her through the living room, past the television, and noticed the game show had ended, and some pitchman was selling pressure cookers. She led me to a closet, where boxes were stacked from floor to ceiling.

"Each of these boxes is filled with pictures of 8th Street. Harry would spend all day snapping away, for over fifteen years, hoping she would return." Her gaze went to the stacks of boxes. "I swear, had he lived, he would still be out looking for her. Take a look."

I lifted the lid of one of the boxes and saw one random shot after another. At that moment, I knew exactly how Harry felt. It had only been days for me, but poor Harry had spent years looking for her.

I swallowed hard before I tried to speak. "So . . . so did Harry ever see her again?"

"Never did. And if you don't stop this nonsense, the same will happen to you."

I closed the box and took a step back. "My case is different. I've never met the lady."

"That may be true, but I know that look in your eyes. She's already got her hooks into you just from the photos."

She walked me out the front door. "Mrs. Summerfield, do you think she'll return?"

"Don't know, and don't care. The best advice I can give you is to get rid of those photos and forget about her. If you don't, she'll destroy you like she did Harry. I've wasted enough of my life on that woman. Good day."

She slammed the door so hard that the glass in the picture window shook. I heard the volume on the television go up as I went down the steps. When I got to my car, I could hardly breathe. Harry had been my best hope of finding her, and he was dead.

Now, this is where any reasonably intelligent person would forget about this and go back to his life, but that was impossible for me. This girl ignited such a fire in my gut that I had to find her, so I turned the car around and went home to look for the person who had taken the 1983 photo.

After long days of searching, I finally gave up. There was no trace of that guy anywhere. All I had left was the name of the 1963 photographer. I knew finding him alive would be a miracle. That photo was taken over sixty years ago, but I was desperate and had to try.

It took me almost six weeks to locate him. Wilber Slater was living in an assisted living complex in Connecticut. I've never prayed for anyone's mental competence before, but I did for Wilber. I called the center, and they transferred my call to his room. I was thrilled to hear how alert he was, and he agreed to meet the following day.

I found him in a wheelchair in the common area. He was a frail little man with horned-rimmed glasses and looked to be asleep.

"Mr. Slater." He raised his head and gave me a questioning look. "I'm Mark Leonard. You agreed to meet me today."

"Oh, yes, I remember. Pull up a chair, young man, so we can talk."

I sat down across from him. "Thank you for seeing me."

"No, no, the pleasure is mine. I don't get many visitors anymore. My wife has passed, as well as most of my friends. My kids live so far away that they rarely get to visit. It's good to talk to a person once in a while who has their own teeth and isn't drooling."

Apparently, his sense of humor was still intact.

"You said from your call that you were working on a story?"

I took out my tablet. "Well, yes and no. Actually, I'm looking for someone. Can I ask you about this image you took, dated September 9th, 1963?"

Mr. Slater took the tablet into his trembling hands, adjusted his glasses, and studied the image tenderly. After a long moment, a smile spread across his lined face. "She's a beauty, isn't she?"

"Yes, she is." I scooted to the edge of my seat. "I realize that was taken years ago, but do you recall anything about that girl?"

He looked up from the tablet. "She's the embodiment of every man's dream and the source of his demise."

I paused momentarily before asking my next question. I knew my search would be over if he said no. "I was hoping you could recall something about her."

"Son, I remember everything about that day. I was focused on that shot when she stepped into the frame. After I snapped her picture, we chatted. I suddenly forgot why I was there and invited her to join me for coffee. She agreed, so I packed my gear and took her to a small café. We talked for hours. She was so mesmerizing I couldn't take my eyes off of her. Finally, she noticed the sun had gone down and said she had to go." He pressed his aged hand to the side of his face. "I can still feel the softness of her lips on my cheek when she kissed me and whispered goodbye."

"Do you remember her name, where she lived, worked, anything that might help me find her?"

He began to laugh. "What makes you think she's still alive?"

I wasn't expecting that question and had to think fast. "Well, you are, so she could be too."

"Her name is Victoria. I have no idea where she lived, but she said she worked at a shop off 8th Street called Freemont's Emporium."

I got my notepad and wrote Victoria and the store's name. "Do you recall her last name?"

"She didn't give it."

"Did you happen to go by her store after your visit?"

He looked at the photo and sighed. "Of course I did, but it

82

wasn't easy to find. I finally found a shop called Freemont Clothing and talked to an elderly man behind the counter. He gave me a funny look when I asked him if this was Freemont's Emporium. He said it hadn't been called that in over seventy years. After his grandfather died in 1918, his father changed the name to Freemont Clothing. His children had other careers, so he was closing the shop at the end of the year."

"Why did she call the shop Freemont's Emporium in 1963 if it was changed in 1918?"

"I've asked myself that question for years." He chuckled softly. "I have to tell you, I was so smitten I kept searching for her for over two years."

"Why did you stop?"

"I came home one night and found my sweet wife with her bags packed. She gave me a choice. Her, or this girl I was hunting. I'm sorry to say it took me a few seconds to choose her." He shook his head. "And thank God I did. I can't imagine my life without Emma." He leaned forward in his chair. "If you don't let this go, your wife will make you do the same."

"Oh. I'm not married."

"And you never will if you let Victoria consume you. You won't be able to love anyone but her. Trust me, I know."

"You felt that way after only a few hours?" He handed me my tablet.

"Son, I was head over heels in love with her after a few seconds."

I shut down my tablet. "That's the second time I've heard something like that."

"Then you should listen." Slater muffled a yawn.

"I won't keep you, sir. Thank you for your help."

"My pleasure, young man." A smile crossed his dry, cracked lips. "If by some miracle you find her, tell Victoria I said hello."

"I will be happy to."

I left Connecticut wondering why he asked me to say hello after telling me to stop looking for her. But look where? I was almost out of time, and all I had was her first name. I only had ten days left to find her. If I didn't, I wasn't certain my heart would survive. How was it possible to be so consumed by a person I had never met?

I arrived on 8th Street before daylight the next morning and set up my camera. I took pictures of every woman I saw and didn't stop until dark. I packed up, went home, downloaded the images, and spent most of the night going through every photo, then repeated the same thing every day after.

"Where are you, Victoria?" I whispered as I set up my tripod on the tenth day. I positioned my Nikon D-SLR camera exactly in the same spot where the last photos were taken and started snapping.

It was late in the afternoon when my attention was diverted by the jarring ring of my cell phone. It was my editor. I'd been avoiding her calls for the last three weeks and knew I had to answer. I switched the Nikon to video mode, turned away from the camera, and answered.

"Hello, Gwen. Sorry for not returning your calls."

"You're four months past your deadline, Mark. J.P. is fed up with my excuses for you being late."

"I know, but I've been working on my next project."

"There's not going to be a next project, Mark. J.P. is demanding you return your advance, or he'll sue."

I shook my head. "Gwen, I don't have it. Tell J.P. I'll have the book to you by the end of the month, and it will be great." There was a long pause. "Gwen, are you there?"

"Mark, you're good, but J.P. won't wait that long. You know how he is. One negative comment from him in the publishing world, and you're done."

"Then I'll have it for you in a week, I swear."

"I'm not sure he'll care."

"Please, Gwen. Tell him if he gives me one more chance, I promise never to miss a deadline again." I started sweating when she didn't answer.

"I'll try, but if I don't have that book in seven days, it's over for both of us. J.P. will take my job and your career."

"Thank you, Gwen. You'll have it, I promise. You're the best."

"Don't thank me yet. Just get me the damn book." She ended the call.

I returned to my Nikon and saw that it had stopped recording. I checked the battery meter, and it showed it was dead. "Damn it. What is wrong with me?" Completely disgusted with myself, I knew then that I had put my career in jeopardy over a ghost.

I packed my equipment, went to my apartment, put my gear away, and logged onto my computer. I barely ate, showered, or slept for the next six days.

I emailed the file to Gwen the morning of the seventh day,

and a few minutes later, she messaged me to say she got it, along with her thanks. I managed to make it to the sofa before I collapsed.

I spent months grieving for a woman I would never meet. I knew she was gone, but I still had to fight the urge to find her. It took another month just to take my Nikon camera out of its case. My first thought was to erase the card file and my downloads and be done with it, but I couldn't bring myself to do it.

This is stupid. You've spent the last three years on this project and collected thousands of images. Just format the 8th Street project and show J.P. the book. If he says no, try a different publisher or do it myself.

I connected the camera to my Mac and downloaded the entire file from the camera. I sat clicking through my files for hours before I reached the first frame of the video. I clicked on the arrow and leaned back in my chair to watch.

Partway through, I jumped up and froze the frame. There she was. So beautiful I couldn't breathe. Her smile was hypnotic. She seemed so real I touched the screen, fully expecting to feel the warmth of her skin. Her face filled the entire screen, and her eyes looked straight into mine. It took a while for me to notice that she was saying something, so I went back to the start of the video, increased the volume, and leaned in. I heard myself talking in the background and saw her eyes trail off from the camera. She was watching me.

"Damn it! Why did I take that call?"

I glanced at the video progress bar and saw it was nearing the end. "She's right there, stupid! Turn around!"

She leaned in and looked directly into the camera. "I've been watching you take photographs on this corner for days. I know this sounds crazy, but I've had a strong feeling we're supposed to meet. Now that I'm here, I wish I hadn't waited so long. I would love to stay and talk, but you're busy, and there's someplace I have to be."

She blew a kiss. "Goodbye, Mark." The screen went black.

* * *

That was five years ago, and I've never stopped thinking of her. During this time, I self-published the book based on all the photos, but instead of calling it *The History of 8th Street,* I titled it *The History of Victoria.* The book was a tremendous success.

Click, Click

I've since written three New York Times bestsellers based on my search for her, which has taken time away from finding her. But that stops at the end of every August. From September 1st to the 10th, I'm on the corner of 8th Street with my camera, taking photos, and I'll continue to do it year after year for as long as it takes. I would gladly give up all my success to be part of her life. Even if it's only ten days every twenty years.

Time has no meaning without her.

Why I Wrote this Story

The idea of this story came to me about seven years ago after taking photographs for my website. In one image, I'm holding a coffee table book published by my brother, Darrell Chitty. Darrell is a gifted artist and photographer near Shreveport, Louisiana. The supernatural element of my story came from my love of the movie *Somewhere in Time*. The rest is history.

Map Maker
Patricia Taylor Wells

James Robert Taylor's life was about to change. He had never been anywhere other than the East Texas community where he was born. But he was also smart and graduated high school when he was only sixteen. His father was a lawyer who owned a land and title plant and hoped his son would follow in his footsteps. Jim, as he was called, enrolled in a small college nearby, but he was immature and didn't like to study. Eventually, he dropped out of school and went back home. His father began teaching him everything there was to know about running an abstract plant, including how to survey land and draw maps.

Once World War II was underway, all men between 18 and 64 were required to register for military service. Jim voluntarily enlisted in the U.S. Army, happy to learn that due to his map-making skills, he was assigned as a Technical Sergeant, and his deployment overseas would be delayed while he trained in the States.

Eventually, Jim was deployed to New Guinea, where he served in the Sixth Army under Lt. General Walter Krueger. The Pentagon was planning an invasion of Luzon, the largest island in the Philippines. At three o'clock each afternoon, Jim would disappear to the Map Room adjacent to Army Headquarters to work on the top-secret maps detailing the military installations that agents and Pilipino guerrillas gathered daily for the invasion.

After slipping through the Finance Department, where the payroll cash was kept, the guards would lift a tarp that opened to the Six Army Headquarters Situation Room. From there, other guards opened the door to the Map Room, where Jim would work solo for two to three hours updating the maps for the invasion. He was involved in other Army intelligence matters the rest of the time.

Map Maker

The temperature in New Guinea was often as high as 115 degrees Fahrenheit. Despite the heat, General Krueger had ordered all his soldiers to keep their collars and sleeves buttoned to prevent bites from poisonous insects, which could be just as lethal as the enemy's weapons. One day, Major Charles A. Willoughby, General Douglas MacArthur's Chief of Intelligence, stopped by to look at the maps. He noticed Jim was sweating profusely despite his efforts to conceal his discomfort. At the major's request, Lt. General Krueger allowed Jim to strip down while working on the maps as long as no one else was in the room.

There was a big meeting after it was determined that the invasion of the Philippines would not take place at Mindanao, the southernmost of its large islands, but at Leyte in the central Philippines instead. The meeting included General MacArthur, Lt. General Krueger, Vice Admiral Thomas C. Kinkaid of the U.S. Seventh Fleet, General George C. Kenney of the U.S. Fifth Army Air Force, two U.S. Senators, and three U.S. House Representatives. Jim had been told to remain quiet and not repeat anything he heard if anyone entered the Situation Room that adjoined the Map Room.

General MacArthur was eager to show off the maps prepared for the invasion, not knowing that Jim was in the next room. Jim froze as the general threw open the huge doors, expecting a room full of laughter when the group saw him in his underwear. Instead, everyone was as quiet as a church mouse. General MacArthur jumped in front of the group, proclaiming, "This is a uniform that I have authorized for this young soldier only when he is working in the Top-Secret Map Room in the Southwest Pacific."

General MacArthur then looked directly at Jim and said," You are not a field grade officer, so I must ask you to leave." A bit embarrassed, Jim quickly gathered his clipboard, uniform, shoes, and gun.

As he left the room, one of the Congressmen stopped Jim and asked if he could shake his hand. "Young man, where are you from?" he asked.

"Texas," replied Jim, struggling to shake hands while carrying his belongings.

"Oh, shoot," said the disappointed Representative who had hoped for a story and photo opportunity to share with his constituents back home.

In July 1944, General Douglas MacArthur and Admiral Chester Nimitz flew to Hawaii to meet with President Roosevelt to discuss the strategy for invading the South Pacific Islands under Japanese control. General MacArthur was determined to restore the honor of himself and the American people from the time President Roosevelt ordered him, his family, and staff to leave the Philippines because the Japanese had surrounded them and would likely try to assassinate the general. On the other hand, Admiral Nimitz was focused on leapfrogging the smaller islands north of the Mid-Pacific.

Now that the Philippine invasion point was officially changed from Mindanao to Leyte, Jim had to rush to make a new map since the planned invasion was less than a month away. Out of the clear blue sky, Jim spotted a Magnolia Petroleum Company roadmap of Leyte, which saved the day. He used this map and the aerial photos the Fifth Army Air Force provided to overlay the coordinates the Sixth Army would use for the invasion. Later, on September 24, Navy pilots under Admiral Marc Mitscher bombed the central Philippines and conducted photographic surveillance around Leyte.

On October 13, 1944, the convoy carrying troops, supplies, and equipment left Hollandia in New Guinea for the Gulf of Leyte. It would take ten days to reach their destination. Vice Admiral Thomas C. Kinkaid took over as the fleet commander of the amphibious command ship USS Wasatch on October 14. Lt. General Walter Krueger was also aboard. Although he was only a staff sergeant, Jim and three other enlisted men from the Six Army were also on the ship headed for the Philippines.

Jim did not begin receiving enemy installations and other information by radio until the fifth day of the journey. Once, when Jim was updating his maps inside the command center of the Wasatch, Vice Admiral Kinkaid stopped by to see how things were going. The admiral picked up one of the maps lying on the desk.

"Where did you get this?" asked the admiral.

"I made it," said Jim. "I used aerial photos and a Magnolia Petroleum Company roadmap of Leyte."

"The Navy doesn't have a map of Leyte as good as this. Do you mind if I borrow your map for a couple of days? I want to add the Navy grid to it."

"Yes, sir," Jim nodded. There wasn't anything he could do but give the admiral the map.

A day later, Vice Admiral Kinkaid returned the map and showed Jim how to use the Navy Grid Calculator to pinpoint target positions by overlaying a template on the grids of the map.

Map Maker

Jim's map was on a large table where five Navy officers with headphones sat as they communicated with aircraft carriers and battleships, sending the enemy targets Jim gave them to the planes in the air.

Once the Wasatch reached its destination on the morning of October 20, it stood offshore, serving as the nerve center for the operation underway. General Douglas MacArthur was nearby on the USS Nashville, waiting and watching as the troops landed on Leyte Island. A little later, the Navy officers on the Wasatch took off their headphones. Jim gave them a puzzled look.

"We're in recess," explained one of the officers. "The planes will still be flying. The war will resume in a couple of hours."

No one mentioned that General MacArthur, his key staff, the Philippine President, Sergio Osmena, and several reporters had boarded a landing craft and were heading for Red Beach on Leyte Island. Upon arrival, General MacArthur and his entourage waded ashore in knee-deep water despite enemy fire heard nearby.

General MacArthur broadcast his declaration to the Philippine people over a radio transmitter, "By the grace of Almighty God, our forces stand again on Philippine soil…" Jim and the others on the Wasatch listened to his speech on the mess hall radio. Afterward, they returned to work. General MacArthur waded ashore the next two mornings at different beaches, repeating his promise to return to the Philippines and garnering additional photo shots of his vainglorious achievement.

Later in the late afternoon on October 20, Jim felt the Wasatch move. He feared the worst and wondered what was happening. Once again, the Navy officers removed their headphones.

"The war is over for us today," one of the officers stated. "We will return when the war resumes at eight o'clock in the morning."

The Wasatch, the Nashville, and three destroyers went out to sea to maneuver with the aircraft carriers for the safety of General Douglas MacArthur. The ships did not return until the following morning. The maneuvers continued for the next two nights. On the fourth night at sea, Jim and the other enlisted men had to sleep in the ship's hold, where food and other supplies were kept, mainly due to the large number of war correspondents on board. Jim slept on flour sacks and showered in salt water, while the reporters had beds and showered in water distilled by the ship's evaporators.

Around midnight on October 24, Lt. General Krueger's Deputy Chief of Staff, Colonel George Decker, awakened Jim and the others sleeping in the hold. The Japanese had come through the Surigao Strait and attacked the U.S. Seventh Fleet. Vice Admiral Kinkaid ordered Lt. General Krueger, the enlisted men from the Sixth Army, General MacArthur, and the war correspondents to go ashore. The admiral took over the USS Nashville and headed out to confront the enemy, relying heavily on PT boats armed with torpedoes to defeat the Japanese fleet. And while General MacArthur kept his promise to return to the Philippines, many were caught in the throes of war because of it. The Battle of Leyte Gulf will long be remembered as the Pacific War's Greatest Naval Battle in history.

James Robert Taylor (Tec3 Staff Sargeant) was awarded a Bronze Star for his service in the Pacific and three other medals. When the war ended, Jim returned home unscathed, other than the invisible wounds many war veterans carry with them for the rest of their lives.

Why I Wrote this Story

One year before my father's death, I interviewed him as he told this story. For many years, the video I taped was lost. I decided to write the story as best I could. I was surprised when I opened a drawer and found the video. There are so many inspiring stories that many have never heard, which is why I am sharing my father's contribution to World War II.

BATTLE IN BURUNDI

DENITA POWELL MALVERN

Battle in Burundi
Denita Powell Malvern

I was born in Tanzania, Africa. My parents and grandparents were born in Burundi. Growing up, we learned about our ancestors' early life in Burundi. For nearly 2000 years my people, the Hutu, lived in peace with the Twa. Seven hundred years ago, the Tutsi came from the Nile region and began to inhabit our lands. The Tutsi were herdsmen, and they brought cattle with them. The Tutsi were quite different. We lived off the land and raised crops. The Tutsi thought our lifestyle was primitive. We lived in Rugos or "huts" and the Hutu began to accept some of the Tutsi customs and traditions.

After school, my grandfather would tell us stories about the battles between the Hutu and Tutsi. We learned that in 1972, my grandfather moved his family to Tanzania because many Hutu were being killed by the Tutsi. Grandfather told us that despite the battles between the Hutu and Tutsi, he wanted to return home. My mother and father were afraid and never wanted to talk about their life in Burundi. "Father, we can't go back you know how dangerous it is," my mother reasoned, "don't you remember what happened to Jacques? What do you think will happen to us if we return to Burundi?" I found out that before my family moved to Tanzania my Uncle Jacques was attacked by Tutsi soldiers. My uncle had just finished a meeting with other Hutu men who were discussing ways for the Hutu to gain more power in Burundi. After the meeting, my uncle was stopped by Tutsi forces. Fortunately, a group of Hutu men in the area aided my Uncle Jacques and the Tutsi soldiers fled. When my uncle Jacques was escorted home, my grandfather packed up their belongings and fled to Tanzania. Many people were able to leave Burundi safely. Sadly, there were thousands of families that could not leave the divided country.

I still didn't understand why the Hutu and Tutsi hated each

other so much. "Grandfather why are the people so angry," I inquired. "My dear little one," my grandfather answered, "for many years Germany and Belgium had control of our land. They did not want peace between the Hutu and Tutsi, so they gave the Tutsi control over Burundi and the Hutu people. The Hutu became very angry and tried to fight back against the Tutsi. Both the Hutu and Tutsi are responsible for a great deal of sadness in our homeland.

In 1992, I celebrated my fourteenth birthday. My parents had finally agreed to move back to Bujumbara, Burundi. There was still great violence in the country, and we stayed close to each other. My father began working at the University and I was enrolled at a nearby school. I attended a school with both Hutu and Tutsi students. Being in Burundi was a big adjustment for me. I was dressed like everyone else. I looked like everyone else. But I spoke differently. The children in my class would tease me because I grew up speaking Swahili and only a little English. I did not know Kirundi or French very well – even though my grandfather tried to teach me the Burundi language several times before.

One day, I was walking home, and I heard a voice calling out from behind me. "Marie, Marie, please wait! I can help you with your Kirundi if you would like?" I noticed that it was Jean-Pierre, a Tutsi boy from my class. I looked at him and asked, "Why would you want to help me? Don't you consider me an outsider?" "Marie, I have felt like an outsider all of my life," he said, "My father is a politician, and he is trying to find a way to bring the Hutu and Tutsi together. The other Hutu students do not like me, and my Tutsi friends tease me because of my father's work. I would like to help you as much as I can," Jean-Pierre continued.

As Jean-Pierre and I continued to talk I learned that his mother was Hutu and that some of his relatives were hurt and killed because of the fighting between the Hutu and Tutsi. Jean Pierre's family also fled to Tanzania, and they returned to Burundi a few years ago. I knew how strongly my family felt about the Tutsi and I wasn't sure if accepting Jean-Pierre's offer was a good idea. I don't remember why, but I agreed to let Jean-Pierre assist me with my Kirundi.

For weeks, Jean-Pierre helped me with my Kirundi and French. I was getting better at speaking the language, but I still had a great deal to learn. Eventually, Jean-Pierre and I became great friends.

A year later, Melchior Ndadaye was elected president and formed the first Hutu government in Burundi. My Kirundi and French had improved so much that I was no longer considered an outsider. There was still tension between the Hutu and Tutsi, but my family learned to survive. Jean-Pierre and I wondered what would happen to Burundi with the new President in office. We hoped that this would bring about change in the country. Shortly after he took office, President Ndadaye was assassinated and the killings in Burundi got worse. The Hutu people blamed the Tutsi for the assassination and attacked the Tutsi. And the Burundian army – controlled by the Tutsi - responded to the Hutu attacks with more violence. My parents did not allow me or my brother Danke to go to school for almost two weeks. We stayed in our home and hoped that the fighting would stop. My brother Danke grew increasingly upset over the battles in Burundi. He told my parents that he was going to stand up against the Tutsi forces like my Uncle Jacques had done so many years ago. My mother burst into tears, and I stared at my brother with fear. I thought to myself, what if he hurt Jean-Pierre, he is a Tutsi and he is my friend.

My grandfather reached for my brother Danke. "My dearest boy, grandfather motioned, "you must calm yourself. If you leave the house now you might do something foolish. You may be seriously injured or killed." Danke ran from my grandfather and headed towards his bedroom. We were all angry about the violence and wanted peace in our homeland.

Just before night fall, there was a knock at the door. "Stay back, we must be careful. The Tutsi forces could be making a night raid," my father cautioned. As my father opened the door I could see Jean-Pierre leaning against the doorpost. His face was bruised and there were traces of blood on his shirt. I ran to Jean-Pierre with terror in my eyes. "Jean-Pierre, what has happened to you," I screamed. Jean-Pierre looked up at me as he mumbled a few words in a tone that I could not hear. My mother ran from the kitchen with a wet towel in her hand. "Winston," my mother called to father, "carry him to the couch and lay him down." My father carried Jean-Pierre to the couch. "Marie, bring a glass of water for Jean-Pierre," my mother insisted. I hurried to the kitchen as fast as I could. I handed the glass to my mother and waited for further instructions. Mother gently raised Jean-Pierre's head and encouraged him to drink. Jean-Pierre swallowed hard and began to speak, "My family is in trouble you must help me. The Hutu forces have attacked several Tutsi families in the area. The re-

Battle in Burundi

bel forces are nearing my parents' home. Please, you must help them. After listening to Jean-Pierre I stood there frozen, unable to move. I was so nervous that I did not notice Danke walking up behind me. Danke spoke with a loud voice, "we will help you." My grandfather smiled and nodded approvingly towards my brother Danke. My father hugged my mother, Danke, and I. "Winston, what are we going to do, my mother asked. "Fanta," my father replied, "prepare the room and make provisions for Jean-Pierre. Danke and my father grabbed a few garden tools and left our home. We sat quietly hoping that Danke and my father would return without harm. Many hours had passed, and it was getting late. Suddenly, there was a loud knock at the door. My grandfather slowly opened the door, and my father and Danke were standing there. Jean-Pierre's family was close behind them. My mother escorted them all to the hidden room where they rested for the night.

The Hutu and Tutsi battled each other for many months. Jean-Pierre and his parents stayed with us until the violence stopped – they were safe. We were Hutu and Tutsi in one home, and we were a family.

Why I Wrote this Story

When I entered college, I developed a deep appreciation for Africa and the vast diversity of its regions. I was inspired by the continent's rich history and deeply saddened by the internal strife of some of its countries – particularly, Rwanda and Burundi. I recall reading a newspaper article about the war-torn countries and wanted to learn more about the Hutu and Tutsi people. **Battle In Burundi** is my first attempt to get more people interested in learning more about the complexities of African countries, often due to colonization and an imbalance of power.

SHADOWS OF THE ECLIPSE

UNRAVELING FEAR'S MONSTROUS GRIP

B Alan Bourgeois

Shadows of the Eclipse:
Unraveling Fear's Monstrous Grip
B Alan Bourgeois

Excitement buzzed in the air as the unique eclipse approached, and Dennis and I were eager to witness this extraordinary event. Unlike many who viewed it through the lens of religious prophecy or doomsday predictions, we sought to experience its spiritual significance in a more profound way. Opting for a dose of DMT to enhance our perception, we prepared to embark on a journey of exploration and enlightenment.

As the sun and moon aligned, casting their celestial spectacle upon the world, Dennis and I found ourselves nestled on the grassy expanse of our apartment complex. With blankets draped around us, we indulged in the calming effects of the DMT, allowing ourselves to sink into a state of deep relaxation.

As the moon began its gradual descent, obscuring the sun and enveloping the world in shadow, we felt a sense of anticipation building within us. It was a moment of profound connection with the universe, a merging of light and darkness that seemed to transcend the ordinary.

In that fleeting moment, as we sat bathed in the glow of the eclipsed sun, we felt a profound sense of unity with the cosmos. It was a reminder of the beauty and wonder that exist beyond the confines of our everyday lives, a glimpse into the vast expanse of the unknown.

As the moon gradually slid across the sun's path, we felt ourselves sinking deeper into relaxation, allowing the effects of the DMT to transport us to another realm of consciousness. Around us, fellow residents of our complex gathered on the common lawn, drawn by the rarity of the celestial event unfolding above.

As the moon reached its zenith, obscuring the sun's rays completely, a subtle shift in the atmosphere caught our attention. What had initially been a tranquil experience suddenly took on a disconcerting edge. An unsettling energy seemed to pulse through the air, causing a ripple of unease to prick at our senses.

Before the eclipse reached its full intensity, we became acutely aware of movement in the shadows, something sinister lurking just beyond the veil of darkness. Our hearts quickened as grotesque figures emerged from the depths, their monstrous forms charging towards us with terrifying speed.

Within mere feet of me, I caught sight of sinister red eyes glaring down, sending shivers down my spine. Panic seized me as I witnessed Dennis springing to his feet and bolting away with surprising speed, despite his usual lack of physical fitness. A monstrous entity, resembling a colossal worm with jagged fins protruding from its back, pursued him relentlessly, devouring anyone unfortunate enough to cross its path.

Meanwhile, another creature of immense proportions, reminiscent of Godzilla, loomed over the scene, its talon-like claws snatching up unsuspecting victims and consuming them whole. As I turned to flee from the approaching horror, I struggled to match Dennis's pace, hindered by the metal in my legs. Each step was a laborious hobble, a desperate attempt to escape the encroaching terror.

As the green-eyed monster drew nearer, its voracious appetite became apparent as it indiscriminately devoured people one by one. This couldn't possibly be the envisioned rapture of Christianity; it was too horrifying, too surreal to comprehend. Yet, despite Dennis and my frantic attempts to flee, others remained frozen in place, transfixed by the celestial spectacle unfolding around us.

In my mind, a frantic plea echoed, urging them to flee, to escape the impending doom. Why were they immobilized, seemingly oblivious to the imminent danger? It perplexed me further when I realized that not everyone was taken by the monstrous entities. Some groups saw only a fraction of their members consumed, while others remained unscathed. The arbitrary nature of the attacks left me bewildered and terrified, questioning the underlying cause of this feeding frenzy.

I was overwhelmed by the chaos unfolding around me. Clothing rained down from above, puzzling everyone as they gradually realized people were vanishing. Panic set in, screams pierced the air, and some even began to prostrate themselves, as if expecting some ominous force. It felt surreal, unfathomable. How could monsters snatch away individuals, leaving others untouched? The logic escaped me. Why were they taken? I struggled to calm my-self, to comprehend. I ran to Dennis who was laying on the ground, drained by exhaustion and terror. Approaching him, I tried to steady my breath. "What just happened?" I demanded, desperation tainting my words. His gaze met mine, filled with the same bewilderment. "You saw it too, didn't you?" I nodded mute-ly. "I don't understand," he confessed, echoing my own confusion.

Dennis, sprawled on the ground, uttered in a weary tone, "I can't make sense of any of it. Why did it choose certain people? Why was it after me? What in the world was happening?" His words echoed my own confusion. As I settled beside him, still struggling to regulate my breath, Dennis attempted to relax and compose himself. Together, we grappled with the events that had just unfolded, trying to piece together the incomprehensible. Gradually, the ominous shadows dissipated with the returning sunlight, revealing the aftermath of the chaos that had erupted in those fleeting moments of darkness. Horrifying creatures had de-voured unsuspecting individuals, leaving behind a scene of bewil-derment and panic. People vanished without a trace, while others remained oblivious to the terror that lurked unseen. Their cries of anguish and confusion filled the air as the realization dawned on them. Where were their loved ones? What had transpired? Some attributed it to a divine act, a rapture of sorts, but for Dennis and me, it was something far more sinister.

Dennis rose to his feet, his gaze shifting from the passing moon to me. He struggled to regain his breath, his mind grappling with the surreal events unfolding before us. Amidst the backdrop of distant screams and frantic calls for loved ones, a chorus of voices cried out, attributing the disappearances to an act of divine intervention. Clothes lay scattered where people once stood, a stark reminder of their absence. "What just happened?" reverber-ated relentlessly in my thoughts as I turned to Dennis, beseeching him for answers. But like me, he was at a loss for explanation. Tremors shook us both as we stood there, surveying the scene, attempting to make sense of it all. Why were we the sole witness-es to the monstrous horrors lurking in the darkness? Why were we the only ones driven to flee while others remained transfixed by the celestial spectacle of the eclipse? For us, it was a night-mare unfolding amidst the beauty, leaving us questioning the very fabric of reality.

The palpable fear between Dennis and me manifested in our

trembling bodies, as though the very ground beneath us quivered in resonance. We felt as if caught in our own miniature earthquake, unable to comprehend the inexplicable events unfolding around us. People who had been there just moments before had vanished without a trace, leaving us bewildered and grasping for understanding. Despite our efforts to steady ourselves, the chaos persisted, leaving us disoriented and shaken. With a collective breath, we silently agreed to retreat indoors, seeking solace and clarity away from the tumult outside. As we ascended the stairs, the echoes of screams and sobbing reverberated, a haunting reminder of the losses endured. Peering out from our vantage point, we observed others emerging from their apartments, their confusion seemed to be mirroring our own, but yet it felt different in confusion. How could they remain oblivious to the turmoil? Why were they spared while others disappeared? The unanswered questions gnawed at us, intensifying our sense of unease. Settling onto the couch, we exchanged tremulous glances, grappling with the unsettling reality of our shared experience.

Dennis entered the kitchen and grabbed a bottle of wine, seeking solace in its contents. As he deftly uncorked it, I retrieved his bag of pot from the bedroom, hoping it would offer some relief from the overwhelming tension. Passing him the pipe, we both took deep drags, desperate to quell our frayed nerves. His hands trembled as he held the pipe to his lips, his gaze mirroring my own bewildered state. "What just happened? What were those creatures?" he uttered, his voice tinged with disbelief. We were both at a loss for words, grappling with the inexplicable events that had unfolded before us. Turning to the television for answers, we found only silence. Channel after channel offered no insight into the chaos we had witnessed, instead broadcasting mundane programs and news reports about the eclipse. Frustration mounting, we toggled through various networks, but the aftermath of the ordeal remained conspicuously absent from the media coverage.

Dennis and I stumbled into the bedroom, sinking onto the bed in exhaustion. Our gazes drifted upwards, fixating on the ceiling as we attempted to process the harrowing sights and emotions that consumed us. However, our minds relentlessly replayed the haunting images of the monstrous entities that had pursued us and others. Thoughts swirled endlessly, questioning why we seemed to be the sole witnesses to these horrific beings emerging from the shadows to prey upon unsuspecting victims. "Why were we the only ones who saw them?" I pondered aloud, the question echoing in my mind as we lay there, grappling with the chilling reality of our shared experience.

* * *

The events of that fateful eclipse day haunted Dennis and me for weeks to come, casting a shadow over our lives that refused to dissipate. We found ourselves plagued by nightmares, reliving the terror of those moments when the world seemed to tilt on its axis and plunge us into a nightmare realm. We sought answers, turning to books, the internet, and even local experts, but no explanation could fully encompass the horrors we had witnessed.

Some nights, I would wake up drenched in sweat, my heart pounding as I remembered the sight of those monstrous creatures emerging from the shadows. Other times, I would find myself staring blankly at the ceiling, grappling with the existential questions that plagued my mind. What were those creatures? Where did they come from? And most importantly, why were we spared while others were taken?

Dennis, too, bore the weight of our shared experience. He withdrew into himself, his once jovial demeanor replaced by a haunted expression. He would often sit for hours, staring into space, lost in thought. I could see the fear in his eyes, the same fear that gnawed at my own soul.

Despite our efforts to move on, the memory of that eclipse day lingered like a dark cloud over our lives. We tried to resume our daily routines, but it was as if a shadow had been cast over everything we did. Simple tasks felt meaningless in the face of such overwhelming uncertainty.

As the days turned into weeks, Dennis and I found ourselves growing distant from each other. Our once unbreakable bond had been strained by the weight of our shared trauma. We would exchange polite greetings and forced smiles, but there was a palpable tension between us that refused to dissipate.

One evening, as I sat alone in my apartment, grappling with my inner demons, I received a call from Dennis. His voice was shaky, filled with a desperation I had never heard before. He asked if he could come over, and I immediately sensed that something was wrong. Without hesitation, I agreed, knowing that whatever demons he was facing, he didn't have to face them alone.

When Dennis arrived, he looked even more haggard than usual. His eyes were bloodshot, and there was a tremor in his hands that he couldn't seem to shake. Without a word, he collapsed onto my couch, burying his face in his hands.

I sat down beside him, placing a reassuring hand on his shoulder. "What's wrong, Dennis?" I asked gently, trying to hide the concern in my voice.

He looked up at me, his eyes filled with tears. "I can't take it anymore," he whispered hoarsely. "The nightmares, the fear... it's consuming me."

I felt a pang of guilt in my chest. I had been so consumed by my own struggles that I hadn't realized how much Dennis was suffering. In that moment, I made a silent vow to be there for him, no matter what.

Together, we talked late into the night, sharing our fears and our hopes for the future. It was cathartic, a release valve for the pent-up emotions that had been building inside us for weeks. And as the first light of dawn broke through the darkness, illuminating the room with its warm glow, I felt a glimmer of hope flicker within me.

The road ahead would be difficult, of that I was certain. But with Dennis by my side, I knew that we would find a way to overcome our shared demons. And as we watched the sun rise on a new day, casting its brilliant rays across the landscape, I realized that sometimes, even the darkest of nights must eventually give way to the light.

But our journey was far from over. Little did we know, the horrors we had witnessed were just the beginning of a much deeper and more sinister mystery that would consume us both.

In that moment, the shadow that had haunted Dennis dissipated, as if swallowed by the returning sunlight. The darkness that had chased him seemed to retreat, leaving behind a sense of relief tinged with lingering fear.

People had vanished, leaving behind an eerie absence that sent chills down our spines. It was as if they had simply been consumed by an invisible force, disappearing without a trace. The realization dawned upon us that this phenomenon was selective, targeting only certain individuals and sparing others. The same as the Christian leaders had been stating as fact of the Rapture in the bible days after the event.

Others grappled with the fear that this was some kind of apocalyptic event, a catastrophic unraveling of the world as they knew it. The uncertainty and terror hung heavy in the air, overshadowing any semblance of understanding.

Dennis and I had made a pact to delve into the mystery of why we were the only ones who could see the monstrous entities during the eclipse. We understood that unraveling this enigma was crucial for our healing process, a necessary step to reclaiming our sanity after the traumatic events of that day.

In our relentless pursuit of answers, we uncovered fragments of stories from survivors scattered across the globe. Their testimonies painted a picture of a world gripped by fear and confusion, where similar events had unfolded in different corners of the Earth. But even with these fragments, the puzzle remained incomplete.

As we connected the dots, a discernible pattern started to surface. It appeared that those who disappeared had a particular quality, a distinct energy that rendered them vulnerable to this mysterious force. Their selection wasn't arbitrary; instead, they shared a common trait that bound them together. And that trait was precisely what endeared Dennis to me the most - his radiance, his infectious joy, a buoyant positivity that naturally attracted others to him in a warm embrace.

With this newfound understanding, Dennis and I embarked on a quest to uncover the origins of this phenomenon. We traveled far and wide, seeking out ancient texts, wise sages, and hidden knowledge that could provide us with the answers we so desperately sought.

Finally, after months of tireless searching, we stumbled upon an ancient manuscript that held the key to unlocking the truth. It revealed that the force that had plagued us was not a divine punishment or an apocalyptic event, but rather a product of human fear and collective consciousness.

The manuscript spoke of a powerful energy that lay dormant within each individual, a force that could be harnessed for both good and evil. It explained that fear, when left unchecked and allowed to grow, could manifest itself in destructive ways, consuming not only the individual but also those around them.

Armed with this knowledge, Dennis and I returned home, determined to confront the fear that had plagued our home. We reached out to the few others that had seen the grotesque monsters, rallying them with hope and resilience. Together, we embarked on a journey of self-discovery and healing, determined to overcome the darkness that had threatened to engulf us.

Through our collective efforts, we learned to face our fears head-on, acknowledging their existence but refusing to let them control us. And as the sun set on the horizon, casting its warm glow across the landscape, we stood together, united in our resolve to never again let fear reign supreme.

Why I Wrote This Story

During the 2024 eclipse in North America, the location I was at was cloudy, preventing us from enjoying a clear view. However, it was the eerie effect of the clouds and the sudden darkness that inspired this story. While this short story explores the theme of 'fear,' it has the potential to evolve into an excellent sci-fi novel one day.

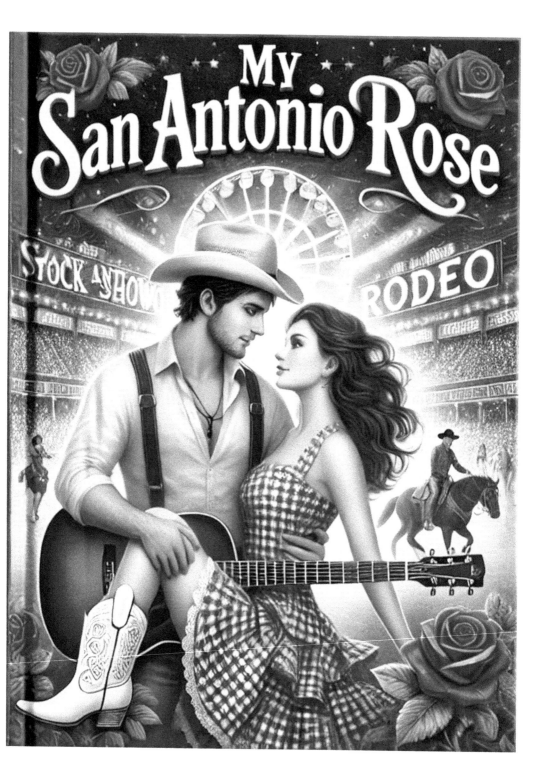

My San Antonio Rose
Vanessa Caraveo

"Kyle! Buddy! I'll be back, and then we'll go. I promise! Are you alright without me?!"

Kyle thought Gage's voice was a little too loud for him, but he understood why Gage was shouting. The deep bass sound system thrummed heavily, and the bright neon lights flashed around the indoor arena as country singer Brad Paisley was performing at the annual San Antonio Stock Show and Rodeo.

"Yes, Gage, I'm good. I'll just…go ahead—"

Gage was already on his way to the dance floor, his blonde-haired company for the night trailing behind him. Kyle smiled and looked around. Many couples with their tall cowboy and cowgirl hats and stylish Western boots occupied the arena's floor, slowly dancing the night away.

Perhaps staying at home practicing his guitar wouldn't have been such a bad idea. He almost had the lyrics for the new ballad he was composing. Not that it mattered much since he hadn't been in a relationship for four years (six months and twelve days, but who's counting?), so there was no one to swoon over anyway. The thought made his throat dry. He needed something to drink, to flush down his reality. He started walking toward the arena's exit when he suddenly stopped, utterly mesmerized, and nearly bumped into a dancing elderly couple who pushed him to the side.

Sitting alone at the bottom of the arena's bleachers was a beautiful girl with long, wavy auburn hair. She had on a red-and-white checkered dress and white western boots. He couldn't see her face, not yet; not all of it at least. But he could see a curve to her lips and would swear he knew how soft her skin was by just looking at it. Kyle was excited for the first time in a long while. A gentle shiver travelled up and down his spine, igniting something inside him.

111

"Well, I'll be damned…" he muttered under his breath. The thirst had disappeared from his throat.

She must have felt his intense stare because she turned his way and gave him the most beautiful smile he had ever seen. It pulled him to her, easily. He could feel his cheeks flush with subtle excitement as he began walking toward her while maintaining eye contact.

"Howdy! Nice to meet you. My name is Kyle. Umm…would you mind having this dance with me?" He held his hand out to her. She looked into his eyes, flashing that gorgeous smile at him once more. Her eyes were bright green, and it felt like she could see right through him. It was both terrifying and lovely.

"I was beginning to think you weren't going to come up to me." She placed her glass back on the table. It was half empty.

"Of course I was." Kyle took in every detail of her face. "I was just waiting for the perfect time."

"So is that now?" She smiled as she ran her index finger around the top rim of the glass. "The perfect time, I mean."

"Dance with me and we just might find out."

Her lips curved into a smile as she took his hand. "Certainly," she responded softly. "My name is Maddie, by the way."

"Kyle."

"Nice to meet you, Kyle."

Kyle could hardly believe what was happening as they made their way through all the couples dancing on the arena floor. They finally found a good spot, and she slowly put her arms around his neck. As he gently placed his hands around her waist, they began to sway back and forth. He could hear Brad Paisley singing one of his favorite songs, "We Danced." He looked down into her bright green eyes. She smiled warmly, looking up into his dark blue ones. This was definitely better than strumming his guitar at home, and he even began feeling a sense of gratitude toward Gage for inviting him to come.

The three songs they danced to felt like pure heaven to Kyle, like a dream he never wanted to end.

"Hey, bud, come on, it's time to go!" Kyle felt a hand on his shoulder. It was Gage, surprised to see Kyle wasn't alone. "Oh, I didn't realize…I'm Gage."

"Maddie."

"Do you think maybe I can call you sometime?" Kyle asked Maddie hesitantly. Gage was insistent on them leaving at that moment.

"I'd love that." She flashed him one last beautiful smile and put her phone number in his phone. They both chuckled, and she gave him a warm hug that weakened Kyle's knees.

* * *

Several phone calls soon turned into dates, and Kyle couldn't get enough of Maddie. They both enjoyed spending time together and learning more about each another. Kyle thought of surprising Maddie with a weekend getaway, just the two of them, hiking at the Friedrich Wilderness Park.

Maddie loved nature, and this park wasn't just big and beautiful, it was known for its rare birds, deep canyons, steep hills, and breathtaking views. He was sure they'd both enjoy the view of the San Antonio skyline. He felt a part of him light up just thinking about showing it to her.

"Whoa, watch your step now," he told her as they finally reached the top of the hill.

"That was a lot harder than I thought," Maddie replied, exhausted as she grabbed her lower back, flinching from pain. She looked up at him and chuckled, then tucked her hair behind her ear. Kyle looked at her, worried about whether she was okay. "It's…Kyle, this is beyond beautiful."

"Right?" Kyle smiled. "I always wanted to bring someone special up here."

Their eyes met for a moment, before Maddie looked away.

"Kyle…there's something I've been wanting to share with you." She seemed nervous as she sat on the hill's ledge and patted the ground next to her.

"Sure, okay." He smiled and sat beside her. "You have my attention."

"It's kind of hard for me to talk about this, but I feel you should know. I was born with a condition called spina bifida occulta."

Kyle stared at her with a confused look. "Spina what…what is that?"

"My spine and spinal cord didn't develop properly before birth. I've had several spinal surgeries to help with this," she said anxiously, looking at the beautiful, serene view in front of them.

She exhaled and continued, "I know it must be a lot to take in, but I assure you I am okay. It's just that doing some physical activities, like hiking or running a marathon, may be hard for me at times."

She turned her backside to him and lifted the bottom of her shirt to show him a scar on her lower back.

"I'm sorry you had to go through that, Maddie. I'm really sorry." He looked at the scar again. He wanted to touch it, but he didn't think that would be appropriate.

"Thanks. I've had a few surgeries to help with issues I have, and I feel truly blessed to be walking today. So many people with this condition are in wheelchairs." Her voice cracked with emotion as she turned back around to look at him.

"The journey to fully embracing myself and how I was born hasn't been easy. There are so many stereotypes about people with disabilities, and since mine is invisible, I always felt it was best just to hide it." She looked up at the skyline in front of them with tears in her eyes.

"I put my trust in the last guy I went out with, and he started getting distant after I told him I had spina bifida. It was clear it was because of that, and I soon regretted sharing this with him." She turned to face Kyle again, her eyes full of emotion. "I just don't want you to see me any differently. It's hard to meet guys who accept me for who I am and understand there are some things I physically may have trouble doing."

He took in a deep sigh and reached out to hold her hands. He looked into those emerald eyes with love and admiration. "Mad, believe me when I tell you it doesn't change how I feel about you. On the contrary, it shows you're a true warrior, and the more I learn about you, the more I admire you. I am so lucky to have someone like you in my life."

Maddie looked into his intense blue eyes with a look of gratitude. "Thank you so much," she softly replied as he gently wiped a tear from her face.

They hugged, embracing the beautiful view and each other's company.

* * *

It was only a short time before they made what they had official and were enjoying even more time together. Kyle was a lot more considerate when planning dates, ensuring that they wouldn't be too physically strenuous, which was something Maddie appreciated about him.

One afternoon, Gage barged into Kyle's room with a flyer.

"Hey, bud, check out this contest. I think it's time for you to be seen!" Gage handed the flyer to him with a wide grin.

"A singing competition? You know I ain't no Keith Urban!"

"You need to stop doubting yourself, man. I've heard how good you are at playing the guitar, and the songs you've composed are awesome. You've got plenty of time to prepare. It's in six months. At least think about it, will you?"

Gage patted Kyle on the back and left.

The next few weeks were quite lonesome for Kyle as Maddie had been busy preparing for senior finals, so they hadn't spent as much time together. She had also started looking at colleges to attend after graduation. Kyle was a proud alumnus of the University of Texas at San Antonio and was pursuing his degree in agricultural economics. He had always been a great student in math, and he also wanted to help his dad with their family's farming business.

"This college doesn't look so bad, and their nursing program has good reviews," Maddie said as she browsed several brochures outside Kyle's front porch one afternoon.

"Come on, sweetheart! I'm going to have to drive an hour and a half to visit you at the University of Texas in Austin." He gave a thumbs down to show his disapproval.

"We can always keep in touch, and you know I'll make time for you on the weekends. I know it won't be easy, but we'll somehow make it work." She put her head on his shoulder. "Gage told me about a singing contest that's coming up next month. I'd be thrilled to see you on that stage. No one can deny you've got talent."

"Nah, only Milo can bear my voice, and that's because he has no choice as my cat," Kyle said, shrugging as Milo rubbed against the porch chair. "Besides, you and Gage know I'm a huge introvert. I don't want to make a fool of myself because of stage fright."

"You know…when I was born, my neurosurgeon told my mother that I wouldn't be able to walk, that I wouldn't make it past my adolescent years, and that if I did, I'd have profound learning disabilities." She got teary-eyed as she spoke. "Something I'll always be grateful for is that despite my mom being a single parent with no support, she never lost hope and always believed in me. This helped me try out things I wasn't sure I could do, and I soon excelled. Doctors told my mom not to let me enter ballet since I might hurt myself. But you think that stopped me?" Maddie stood up to do a perfect relevé in front of him.

"I believe in you, Kyle, and know you can accomplish much if you step out of your comfort zone. Gage and I have heard you sing and play guitar, and you are very talented. You're not meant to just entertain Milo. Others need to hear you, too." She giggled and softly petted Milo's back as he passed by.

"At least consider it for me, okay?" She made a pleading gesture with her hands while giving him the cutest smile.

"I'll think about it." Kyle lightly chuckled as Milo jumped up on the porch chair to plop in his lap.

* * *.

Weeks passed, and the day of the singing contest arrived. Kyle decided to take the risk and try his luck, with his girlfriend, best friend, and family fully supporting him. After thinking about it, he figured it would be a good idea not only to be an agricultural economist but also to be able to do some singing on the side.

"Ladies and gentlemen, we now have contestant number nine, Kyle Henderson!"

The crowd cheered when he was announced, and he could hear Maddie and Gage's loud and encouraging chants.

On stage, he sat on the stool in front of the mic, guitar in hand.

"There's a special song I want to sing tonight for a special person. She's the reason I am on this stage and has inspired me with her strength to believe in myself, showing me that I can overcome anything I set my mind to. To my beautiful San Antonio rose, Maddie."

At that moment, Kyle sang and played his guitar like never before. The crowd cheered him on, enjoying his great cover of a Bob Wills and His Texas Playboys' popular country song. He received a standing ovation, and he truly felt blessed to have shared his talent with those present. He went backstage right after he gave a half bow to the crowd and there he met Gage and Maddie. She was smiling, her arms wide open for a hug.

"I'm so proud of you, honey! You were great!" She hugged

him so tightly he never wanted that moment to end.

"That was a great performance, bud." Gage placed his hand on Kyle's shoulder. "I always knew you had it in you."

"Thanks, guys," Kyle said. "Thank you, really. None of this would have happened without either of you. Thank you."

"You're welcome, sweetie," Maddie said. "Oh, they're about to announce the results."

"Come on, let's go find our seats." Gage led the way back to Kyle's elated parents.

A few minutes later, the emcee opened an envelope after the judges had made their final decision.

"The results are in! And we will now be announcing this contest's winner!"

Kyle and Maddie heard the crowd roar and locked hands.

"Congratulations, contestant number nine! Kyle Henderson, you are the contest winner!" Kyle couldn't believe how excited the crowd was when he went to the front of the stage to accept his trophy and five-thousand-dollar cash award.

The event ended, and Kyle couldn't believe what had just happened. He gathered his belongings backstage and placed his guitar in the guitar case. Suddenly, he felt arms around him, embracing him tightly.

"I'm so proud of you! You were wonderful!" Maddie exclaimed as he turned around to hug her back.

"A rose for a rose." He smiled and handed her a beautiful red rose he had been saving for her.

They lovingly kissed and soon joined the rest of his family. Everyone celebrated his triumph at a festive dinner at home, and he couldn't remember the last time he had felt so much joy and optimism in his life. He had a loving girlfriend, a supportive best friend, and a family who was proud of him. He felt like the king of the world.

* * *

Kyle's and Maddie's families were sitting on the bleachers at Reagan High School, anxious to see Maddie walk down the field as a high school graduate. Despite all the challenges she had needed to overcome in her life, she managed to graduate in the top five percent of her class, and Kyle could not have been prouder of his girlfriend. They cheered her on and, after the ceremony, went back to celebrate at a graduation party her family had thrown for her at home.

The next day, he went to pick up Maddie at home so they could go on a picnic date. It was almost summertime, and the warm and sunny weather was the perfect touch. After eating the delicious food they had prepared, Kyle stretched his legs out on the blanket, and Maddie positioned her head on his stomach.

"I wanted to let you know I've decided what college I'll be attending in the fall, and Texas State University looks like the one for me," she said, giving a thumbs up of approval.

"Glad for you, Mad." Kyle gulped, trying to hold back his emotions.

"We're going to stay in touch every day." She sat up to look at him. "And an hour and a half away isn't too bad."

"I'm going to miss you." He had tears in his eyes.

"Maddie, before I met you, I was just a lonely guy playing guitar at home with no purpose. When you came into my life, you changed the way I see many things and encouraged me to try out new things. You believed in me, which is why I won that singing contest, and I now know I can turn my dreams into reality…It's all because of you."

She gently wiped a tear from his face as he spoke.

"You've inspired me so much, Mad. Knowing all you went through and the medical challenges you've had to overcome since you were little, yet you still remain positive in life, accomplishing all the goals you've set for yourself. I love you so much and am lucky to be with someone like you."

"I love you too." She leaned in to give him a warm hug as tears trailed down her face. "You know…I remember countless nights when I'd pray to God to find a guy who would completely accept me for who I am. Then I met you that night at the stock show dance, and you are everything I could have wished for. You understand and respect me, and your kind heart is truly one of a kind. I love you so much, Kyle."

Kyle slowly leaned in to kiss her and tenderly whispered in her ear, "And I'll always love you, my San Antonio rose."

Why I Wrote This Story

I wrote this story to raise disability awareness and to share the inspiring message that we can all turn our dreams and goals into a reality if we are brave enough to step out of our comfort zone and continue to persevere. Being born and raised in Texas, I wanted my story to have a country setting and pay homage to one of my favorite country songs, "San Antonio Rose" by Bob Wills. I also wanted to provide readers with deeper insight into individuals living with invisible disabilities, such as spina bifida occulta, hearing loss, autism, diabetes, and fibromyalgia, and the many social challenges they face. I believe having characters with disabilities can help readers learn more about various disabilities so that they can better understand these individuals. Through literature, we can help foster a more inclusive society by eradicating the stigma that continues to exist toward people with disabilities.

Texas Authors Institute of History, would like to thank our sponsors and our advertisers for helping us to raise money for literacy.

FREE MAGAZINE

New for
Texas Authors

Designed to Help Authors to Succeed Pre-Publishing, Publishing, Book Marketing & Authors Museum
Available Now
TexasAuthors.Institute

The Sand Rose
PATRICIA TAYLOR WELLS

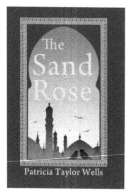

"Only in complete silence will you hear the desert."
Bedouin Proverb

Gaylen Mackenzie, a young, single American woman is offered a position at her company's headquarters in Saudi Arabia. She quickly learns she must confront the challenges of living in a society that largely excludes women from just about every freedom she grew up taking for granted. Adapting to this new world is more than remembering a headscarf when venturing beyond the company compound. But as the Kingdom slowly gives up its secrets, Gaylen learns to appreciate the hypnotic beauty of the desert and Islamic traditions.

Like the delicate sand roses found in the salt flats of the Arabian desert, the author, recalling upon her own experience in Saudi Arabia, reveals the fragile beauty and mystery of a country constructed over the ages from strong and proud traditions.

www.patricia-taylor-wells.com

Books by William Nelson Fox

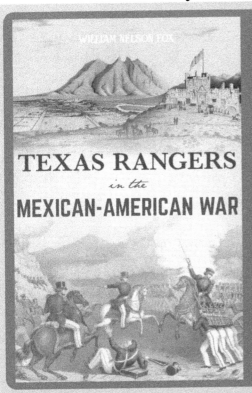

Historical Non-Fiction

"Discover the thrilling and controversial saga of the Texas Rangers during the Mexican-American War, where heroes like Samuel H. Walker, Benjamin McCulloch, and John "Jack" Coffee Hays led the charge and shaped history with their legendary feats in a war of vengeance!"

ISBN: 9781467153867

Available at
Your Favorite Bookstore

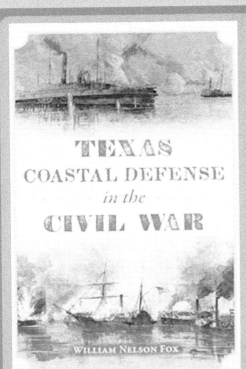

Historical Non-Fiction

While volumes focus on the Civil War, the defense of the Texas coast remains largely overlooked; however, Texans left behind valiantly repulsed naval bombardments and invasion attempts until Federal troops finally entered South Texas towards war's end. In his account, William Nelson Fox highlights both famous battles and obscure skirmishes, detailing the Lone Star State's defensive strategies during the Civil War.

ISBN: 978-1467155618
Available at
Your Favorite Bookstore

Top Ten Author Series

by Multi Award-Winning Author Advocate
B Alan Bourgeois

30 Books Covering

Pre-Publishing   Publishing   Marketing

2024 First Place Texas Best Non-Fiction Business Series

CHANGE THE WORLD SERIES

BY MULTI AWARD-WINNING AUTHOR

B ALAN BOURGEOIS

Politics   Acceptance   Social Awareness

ASB
INDIE AUTHORS
BEST BOOK AWARD
2024
Non-Fiction Series

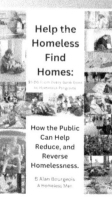

HOW TO BEAT THE QUARANTINE
READ A GOOD BOOK
About *TEXAS*

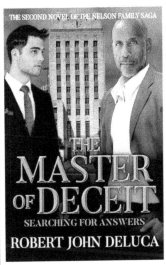

The **Master of Deceit** is the second in the Travis Nelson saga series. In this Houston based thriller, Matt Norton is pitted against a slick but ruthless con man, who in plain sight pulls of an amazing scam on the City and County and then vanishes. Matt is determined to bring him to justice.

Aimed at middle grade readers of all ages, Justice for a Texas Marshall, recounts the continuing escapades of Marshall Morris. Our favorite star-crossed student in a small south Texas high school finds himself ensnared in a high-time college football recruiting scandal. As always, Marshall finds a way to succeed but never takes the obvious path.

These books are available in bookstores, Amazon and the Indie Lector bookstore in paperback and eBook formats. The **Master of Deceit**, which is published under Defiance Publishing imprint, is also available as an audiobook.

Robert John DeLuca

B Alan Bourgeois has an extensive track record of having helped hundreds of authors achieve their publishing goals through a variety of channels, including self-publishing and hybrid models. He is skilled in guiding authors to literary agents that are aligned with their specific needs.

Leveraging his extensive experience in book marketing and sales, as well as his participation in numerous book festivals, library conferences, and writing conferences, B Alan Bourgeois is able to assist authors in identifying and selecting the most suitable events to advance their careers. He further represents his clients at these conferences through his various organizations.

B Alan Bourgeois' consulting services are available to authors at every stage of their writing journeys - from beginners to seasoned professionals seeking new avenues for growth.

BOURGEOIS
MEDIA & CONSULTING
Creative Inspiration Realized

BourgeoisMedia.com

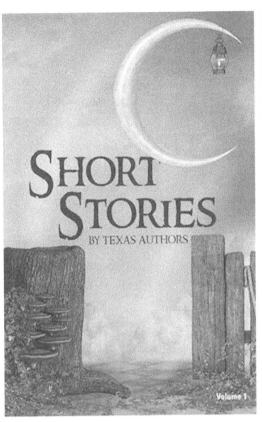

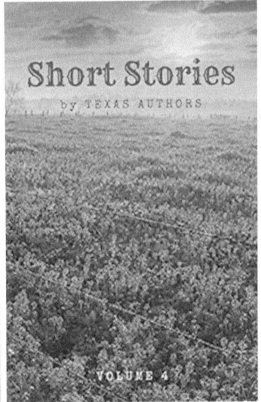

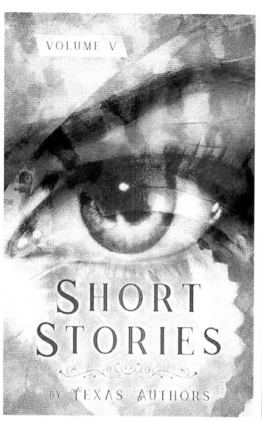

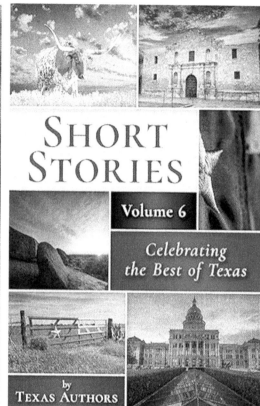

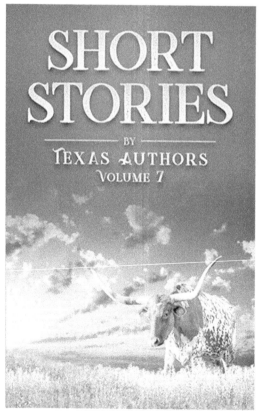

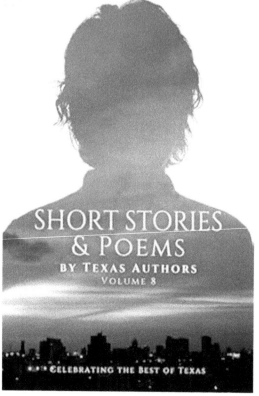